Saffron & Rosewater

her tears and mine changed our lives forever…

JOHN ABRAHAM

First Published in 2021

Becomeshakespeare.com
One Point Six Technologies Pvt. Ltd.
119-123, 1st Floor, Building J2, B - Wing,
Wadala Truck Terminal, Wadala East,
Mumbai 400022, Maharashtra, INDIA
T: +91 8080226699

Copyright © 2021, John Abraham

All rights reserved. Any unauthorized reprint or use
of this material is prohibited. No part of this book
may be reproduced or transmitted in any form or
by any means, electronic or mechanical, including
photocopying, recording, or by any information storage
and retrieval system without express written permission
from the author/publisher.

Please do not participate in or encourage piracy of
copyrighted materials in violation of the author's rights.
Purchase only authorized editions.

ISBN - 978-93-90463-79-4

Saffron
&
Rosewater

John Abraham was born in Kolkata (formerly known as Calcutta) and went to school at Good Shepherd International School (Ooty, India). He completed his graduation from M.G. University (Kerala, India), and later he Post Graduated from the Sikkim Manipal University (India) completing his MBA.

Saffron & Rosewater is his first attempt as a novelist. He is currently working in Dubai (United Arab Emirates), is married to Disna, and is the father of a boy, Ayiedan.

Saffron & Rosewater is about a boy's journey through life who is trying to help his father out of a financial crisis. It talks about how he landed up in the Middle East taking up his family burdens and his hardships. The book talks about the boy's journey to adulthood. It showcases Indian family values and the commitment and obligation children have towards their parents. The book is more about the love and passion which this boy develops towards a woman who comes into his life and who nurtures him to be a successful man.

Disclaimer

This book is a work of fiction. Names of persons, characters, businesses, organizations, places and events are fictional and a product of the imagination of the author. Any resemblance to actual events or places or persons, living or dead, is entirely coincidental. Any reference to hotels, places, businesses, locations and organizations, while real, are used in a way that is purely fictional and has no resemblance to any existing organization, location, etc., and any use thereof is not intended to harm, disrespect, defame or derogate any third party.

To my Mummy & Daddy

For all the beginners and strugglers out there.

For all those who love their Parents unconditionally.

For all those who have been rejected throughout their lives.

For all those who have lost more than they have won.

For those who have lots and lots of LOVE within them and nothing else.

For all those who live and die for LOVE.

Let's spread LOVE.

Thank you, Abba, the Lord my Father
for all the blessings showered upon me.

Acknowledgments

First of all, I would like to thank all the women who had come into my life and had left for various reasons; you have all played a very important role in my life in a way or another. I would like to thank the love of my life; you know who you are...it was you who inspired me to grow every day; I always wanted to do better in life to be good and worthy enough for you; all the best to you my dear.

I would like to thank my wife, Disna, without whom I would not have been what I am today. She has been my driving force and the reason why I dare to dream in colors—the impossible, and her only purpose in life seems to be to see me grow and be successful in whatever I do. This book happened only because of her. She and my son Ayiedan had to sacrifice all their weekends and holidays staying at home doing nothing so that I could sit and write Saffron & Rosewater. Hats off to their patience and encouragement from the beginning till the end. Love you both.

Mr. Venkitesh, my English teacher from Good Shepherd International School (Ooty) (formerly called Good Shepherd Public School), thank you Sir for noticing the writer in me. While most of the teachers were complaining about my academic performance this man was reading out my English composition to my classmates. Thank you, Sir, for encouraging me and for giving me marks generously for what I had written on my answer sheets without any presumptions.

I would like to also thank my Hindi tuition teacher in Calcutta, M.P. Singh Sir, who also saw a writer in me. He used to ask me to write compositions and I always found a story in each of his topics. He would read them and say in Hindi, "I asked you to write a composition but you wrote down a heart-melting story."

My sister, Kavita Sara Abraham, was the one who introduced me to books. She is a book worm, and it was my curiosity to know what she was reading that made me read as well. Thank you for loving and caring for me unconditionally and for being by my side always.

I would like to dedicate this book to my Daddy, Mr. A.I. Abraham, and Mummy, Mrs. Lilly Abraham—the two souls because of who I am in this world today. Thank you for all your blessings.

Whenever I needed a sponsor, I knew whom to turn to, my father-in-law, V. Rev. Varghese Jacob Corepiscopa.

He has sponsored me whenever I required it without a question being asked. Thank you for believing in me and for supporting me always.

A big salute to all the people who have encouraged me in my life, my extended family, nephew and niece, in-laws, my cousins, and to everyone who loves and hates me, thank you for everything.

With that presenting, Saffron & Rosewater.

Prologue

I cannot see my Daddy sitting on the chair at the dining table with his head down doing nothing about our situation.

I cannot see Mummy struggling to think about what she could make for lunch or dinner with the little she had in stock.

I was not going to wait and watch until everything was over.

Daddy, don't worry, it is ok, let everything go... I have got this; you relax. I will take it up from here.

With no clue as to what needs to be done, I set out to save my home and my family at the age of 23.

My Daddy's head should never bow down in front of anyone.

I had to do this myself without anyone's help.

However, I never thought I would see her again in this desert. Her friendship gave me new hopes, new meanings and it changed our lives forever.

Chapter 1

Present-day...

Is it raining?

(*wife*) No!

I thought it was raining... Mummy was saying it was raining back in Kerala when I called her yesterday.

It is only 4:30 A.M. Stephen, sleep for some more time.

Perhaps, the buzz from the air-conditioning and the sound of the water flowing in the fish tank might have given that rain feeling in my head.

My body has got used to the regular 5:00 A.M. alarm for work. It is Friday here in Dubai. It is still dark outside.

It has been 11 years in the gulf, not sure if I have achieved anything so far, but just going on, living, and saying to myself that you are blessed if you have food on your plate, a roof over your head, and clothes to wear then you are rich.

Daddy's business had fallen apart in India. I had to beg my brother-in-law and sister to let me have a place in Dubai to save my house from being sold—the only asset which my Daddy was left with, everything else was invested into their business and the business was no more.

My brother-in-law was my Daddy's business partner as well. However, I am still not sure as to why was I made to suffer by both of them—to finish off the debts which their business had caused. Maybe it was my fate, destiny? Today, my Daddy has no debts. I took care of everything. He is sleeping peacefully in his house, I suppose, with my dear Mummy.

I walked out of my brother-in-law home with 20 dirhams in my pocket. I was tired and had had enough by then. I just could not see my sister suffer because of me and could not take any more insults from her husband.

I stand here today, looking out of the window of my apartment. The sun is rising. I have overcome everything, my proud mind says that "you are a hero!" but my heart knows that I have lost more than I have achieved. There is more pain than the feeling of a winner within me.

I wish I could get a cup of Sulaimani to drink. My wife is sleeping, sleeping peacefully. She is very beautiful. The love of my life, my everything, the one who holds the key to my heart, and the other one is, of course, our daughter.

Let me go and make a cup of Sulaimani (black tea) with saffron, rose water, and a little bit of sugar for myself.

Chapter 2

Day 2 of staying hungry! Having a little water left in my bottle, I stole some more water when the house owner and his wife stepped out of the house. Fingers crossed that they don't find out. If only there are no holidays like these, for it is difficult to stay hungry.

Not having money when you are in another part of the world is a curse. And it feels worse when your own treat you like trash. 20 dirhams was only enough to buy a few essentials; another 15 days for the salary to arrive and it is a holiday in UAE. Most of the families are enjoying, the restaurants are packed with people and the smell of food is in the air and here I am stuck hungry and dejected. Another 2 more days to get back to the office. Holidays means no food; I usually got packed lunch from a small cafeteria located adjacent to my work place for which I had to pay only when my salary came in, nothing fancy just some rice, daal and subji; I used to split that into two portions keeping the second for dinner. I bought a packet of bread for now.

The small room where I stayed as a paying guest was quite more than the regular bachelor's accommodation or bed space. Perhaps, my stomach had stopped grumbling; might have got used to the "no food" concept by now.

When there was so much pain. within there was hope—hope was in my wallet; a small picture torn out of an old school yearbook of Rachel. A picture that was like oxygen to my parched thoughts and food for my soul. A picture that was like music to me. I always wanted to grow up to be worthy of her. We both studied in the same boarding school since grade four back in India.

I fell in love with her when I was in grade eight. She was very beautiful, with a broad forehead, her eyes were big and pretty, her nose was pointed, her lips were like rose petals pink and soft.

She used to sit a few tables away from mine in the dining hall of our boarding school. I used to love looking at her, her smile was like everything to me, it just lit up my mood. I would do anything to impress her. Nonetheless, she never paid much attention. Like all stories, she was very beautiful and popular, and I was the not so popular and not so good-looking guy in our batch.

It was our grade 10th board exams and the night before our Chemistry exam was horrid which I can never forget in my life.

I was sitting on Karti's bed—he was my senior and we were good friends. I was taking a break before I could revise the chemical formulas one last time before getting to bed. Everyone else had already got into their beds after dinner except a few of us who were studying. Suddenly, I was pulled and thrown down on the floor. It was our school Principal, along with Vicky Sir, our Headmaster. The Principal kept kicking on my face with his shoes on. I started bleeding from the eye but he never stopped. He kept disconcerting me using different salutations and kept on yelling and shouting at me on top of his voice. I did not understand a thing that was happening. It all happened so swiftly that I had no clue as to why was I being beaten up or rather being kicked at.

The next day I did not have any breakfast. I walked straight to the ground near our examination hall. After a few minutes, Rachel and her friends arrived; I saw that she was upset. At first, I thought she was upset seeing my swollen eyes but then one of her friends told me that she liked Shanon another guy from our batch and he had rejected her proposal. Those words broke my heart.

As my owners went out and closed the door behind, I came back from my reverie into my horrid present. It was time to rob some water from their kitchen. I quickly kept the picture back into my wallet and opened the door to my room; there was silence everywhere.

I double checked around the house to be sure that no one was around watching, and then went into their kitchen to fill in my bottle from their water dispenser making sure that the level hadn't changed much. I could smell food but didn't have the courage to even touch it.

Chapter 3

Stephen: Hey, Ziya...do you love me?

Ziya: I will answer you once I finish running one more round around the school campus.

Stephen: Can't wait until then, need to go home.

Ziya: Do you really want to know?

Stephen: Ziya!

Ziya: Hmmm....yesss!

Ziya was a very good runner–the pride of this day-scholar school. Ziya is in grade eleven and Stephen was in grade 12.

Ziya dreamt of becoming a famous athlete. She was introduced to me by Michelle; both of the girls were best of friends.

Stephen really liked Michelle a lot, but Rachel would never go away from Stephen's heart. Back in those times, the internet and mobile phones were luxuries, so there was no way to contact Rachel; she was said to be located somewhere in the Middle East.

Michelle was an Anglo-Indian girl, she was pretty, she had big and beautiful fronts and was awesomely sexy. We both had a connection from the beginning, but she was a quiet person, unlike Ziya. Ziya had that zing that matched mine and it was much easier to connect with her, but she was not my kind of a girl.

This school always looked strange to me. It was unlike my boarding school and I always wondered if there was anyone who matched my kind of wavelength. At that age, in a place like Kerala, especially in a remote place like where this school was located, knowing to speak the language English without the traces of your mother tongue coiling through the words was considered cool. I suddenly became the star of that place and getting dropped at school by a driver on my Daddy's car every day made me look like the rich and famous. Those two years were the best days of my life and the years which I would never ever forget.

Every other girl in that school had a crush on me and the only two women I spoke to apart from my classmates were Michelle and Ziya. The best-looking girls in that school at that time indeed! After school time it was a calling session at home. I used to speak to both these girls for hours over the phone. We spoke about so many things, with Michelle it was mostly about love, sex, Ziya's body which was almost transforming into a man's body because of her training regime.

With Ziya, it was more about love, sports, workout, and her future goals.

Ziya was so into her career that she had very little time to talk about anything else, it was always about sports and her goals, but Michelle was a wife material, a very nice girl with whom I could speak anything without any restrictions, be it sex, love or about her best friend's body. She was very understanding, kind, and a real woman in all sense.

But keeping all things aside, Rachel was always a sweet pain in my heart.

All looked good at that age—a "star" acceptance at school, the best girls of the school calling me every night, Daddy's flourishing business, and the standard of life which that could buy; but somewhere within me there was a pain. I really loved Rachel and I always believed that I would marry her someday, everything else, rather every other girl was only secondary. That night I secretly opened up the old album with pictures taken during our farewell day at my boarding school. I looked at the few pictures taken that night, memories... All of us were well-dressed. Rachel was wearing a green sari with red borders. I had clicked a few pictures that night with her which looked like our wedding pictures—just both of us together. That night was the best night I had with her ever. Jimmy and Sahu, my two other best friends, were continuously clicking photos of us both together with my camera. The night was beautiful and unforgettable. Thanks to Jimmy and Sahu, my best friends from the boarding school, who made that night memorable for me.

I closed the album with tears in my eyes, realizing that all I wanted was Rachel and nothing else. I prayed that night to the Lord all mighty. I asked for Rachel; I prayed for Rachel's love.

Kerala is well known for the number of churches it has. I wanted to see and pray at all the churches I had never been to. I told my parents and I was taken to many churches from then on; little did they know what I had in mind and what my tears and prayers were for. My parents were surprised to see the change within me.

There is a myth that if we ask God in prayer for something in a church you are visiting for the first time your wish would be granted. I had only one prayer and that was "Rachel". I believed that my wish would be granted someday. I believed that my love for her would bring her to me. I believed that all the universe would conspire in bringing her to me. I believed that in one of these churches when I had finished praying she would be standing right behind me.

Chapter 4

After finishing my dinner I went into my room to pack my college bag as usual, I had picked to study B.Com after my 12th grade. College was in the city so I had to pack all my books and Mummy used to pack lunch for me every day as I would get back home after college quite late. I had to leave early so that I could use the public transport bus to the city in order to reach college in time. As days passed by, all my friends went different ways after our 12th standard and not much contact was left with any of my friends.

Meanwhile, the phone rang and Daddy picked up the phone. "Hello! Oh hi...how are you son? Yes, Stephen is here...I will call him.

Daddy: Stephen! (calling out loud) Call for you...

Stephen: Hello...

Jimmy: It's me Jimmy...how are you?

Stephen: Hey...Hi...I am good...how about you? Where are you calling from?

Jimmy: I am good...I am here in Kerala...I will be here for 3 days...shall we meet tomorrow?

Stephen: I have college tomorrow...but I will come and see you...

Jimmy: Ok, come to my Uncle's office at Marine Drive.

Stephen: Ok see you tomorrow.

All excited Stephen went to his father who was reading a book...

Stephen: Daddy...Jimmy is here...my old friend from boarding school days. Can I go and see him tomorrow?

Daddy: What about your classes tomorrow then?

Stephen: That's ok I can manage...I will get all the notes copied later.

Daddy: Well if you can manage then go ahead.

Stephen: Thank you, Daddy! Daddy one more thing....

Daddy: What is it now?

Stephen: Can I get some extra money tomorrow (normally only the transportation charges were given to me as pocket money, not a penny more, not a penny less).

Daddy: Why do you want money?

Stephen: Please Daddy...just a bit...please...they are very big people and I should also have some money with me, right?

Daddy keeps aside the book he was reading and gets up from the bed and opens the cupboard where he keeps his money bag, opens it, and hands over 10 currency notes all ten-rupee notes.

Stephen: Daddy the office is in Marine Drive, I will need a little more money for lunch etc., please...

Daddy: hmm

Daddy hands over another 10 more ten-rupee notes– all of them were quite dirty. In fact, he selected the dirtiest notes available in that bag.

Stephen: Thank you.

I was thrilled that I received 200 rupees as pocket money for the first time in my life, but at the same time was upset as most of them were torn and had become thick with dirt on them. The currency that was given to me was so dirty that I thought I had to touch them with gloves. But as the saying goes beggars cannot be choosers, I kept all the notes carefully in my old black faded leather purse. I was waiting to see my old friend and that's what mattered most.

I reached Marine Drive and went into the GCDA complex building where Jimmy's uncle had an office.

The office was Jimmy's father's actually, their Kochi branch. The head office was managed by Jimmy's father in Mumbai.

It was a massive office, air-conditioned rooms, with staff working. I walked to the reception and asked for Jimmy, the receptionist lady replied in a sweet voice, "Are you, Stephen?"

I said, yes. The receptionist pointing her finger at the nearby staircase said, "Sir is waiting for you upstairs, the last cabin to the right."

Jimmy was waiting for me in a cabin in that big office. I suddenly felt uncomfortable. I became aware of the dirty notes in my gluttonous wallet. I hesitated a bit and then decided to knock at the cabin door. Suddenly, the door opened from the other side and Jimmy hugged me with a smile on his face.

Jimmy: At last, after so many years... Sit down, dude; how are you?

Stephen: I am good. So happy to see you...

Then we spoke about our old days at school and all the naughty things we did at school.

Jimmy: I still remember Sally miss. Do you remember her? The one who was short and who had massive tits?

Stephen: Coconuts? (*giggles*)

Jimmy: Yes! (*laughs out loud*) That is the one. Those days were the best days man; I still remember our computer miss.

Stephen: Yeah... We used to shag (our code word for masturbation) in her class while she was teaching us. Gosh can never forget those days.

Jimmy: Remember our shagging competition...(*giggles*)

Stephen: (Laugh out loud) Yeah in those days who ejaculates first used to be considered the winner, when actually it is just the opposite. (*chuckles*)

Jimmy: Have you fucked already?

Stephen: No!

Jimmy: Then how do you know all this?

Stephen: Bro, the more it is delayed the more you are considered a stud.

Jimmy: Hey tell me the truth...have you experienced it already?

Stephen: No man... I just know... The woman needs to be drilled slowly and smoothly in a rhythmic way and the more time you take to ejaculate the more she will enjoy it. (*chuckles*)

Jimmy: Fuck...stop man! My dick is already going on a hop... You were always an expert in these things. I remember you had once told a hot movie story in school... What was the name?

Stephen: *Lady Dynamite?*

Jimmy: Yeah..that one (*laugh out loud*) I still remember guys running to the toilet at the end of the story or maybe in between itself.

Stephen: That was all made up! I don't think there is even a movie in that name. (chuckles)

Jimmy: Sahu was so wet after your story. (*giggles*) Sad that he is no more, wish he was here.

Stephen: I am sure he is here... watching from a distance... smiling

(silence in the room for a minute...)

Jimmy: Hey, Rachel is in Canada now. She is studying there. She is completely changed man; not the old Rachel anymore

Stephen: What do you mean not the old Rachel? How do you know all this?

Jimmy: I have her e-mail address. We chat at times on MSN chat. Oh my god, you should see her now! She comes in front of the webcam with skimpy clothes. She is hot man...

Stephen: E-mail? MSN chat? webcam? What is all that?

Jimmy: I will show you, come...

And then I was introduced to the world of the internet. He showed me how to use the internet. He showed me porn on the internet. All this was new to me and we had to literally wait for so long to see porn pictures together as it took ages to download. He created an e-mail address for me on Hotmail and he showed me how I could chat with Rachel on MSN chat. He also showed me how I could use one of the chat rooms to speak to random people with like minds about topics ranging from sex to whatever. The world of the internet was awesome. It was like my prayers were heard after all. I was going to send Rachel an e-mail. I was going to chat with her. I had mixed feelings about the whole idea, but I was eager to try. What if she starts liking me now? What if we can get together? Will she understand my love? How will I start a conversation?

I kept thinking about all of this the whole night that day and I thanked Jimmy for coming back into my life.

Chapter 5

With a lot of thought, I decided that I was going to send Rachel an e-mail. I went to the internet café near my home and sat on one of the computers there. The rate board outside said "1 hour browsing – Rs 7". Therefore, I quickly switched on the computer and waited for the internet connection to actually get connected. In those days there was only a dial-up connection and after almost 15 minutes it started to work, and I got on to Hotmail and started typing her an e-mail.

e-mail to Rachel

Dear Rachel,

How are you? I hope everything is going well there. I hope you still remember me? I am in Kerala and currently a 1st-year graduate student. I would like to chat with you. Please let me know a suitable time.

Thank you.

With lots of love and prayers

Stephen

Later in the evening, I got back to the internet café again to check if there was any reply and to my surprise, there was a mail in my inbox and it was from Rachel. I quickly opened it.

Reply from Rachel

Hi,

I am very busy in the mornings, but I can squeeze out time at night to have a talk with you.   I will be online tonight. Let's meet there then!

Bye.

That was an unpredictably small e-mail, but I thought to myself that maybe that's the way an e-mail is written? But then chatting at night (Canada time) would mean I will have to be available early in the morning, no internet café opens at 3:00 A.M. or 4:00 A.M. in my place except for one which opens at 7:30 A.M. which was on the way to my college at Manorama Junction.

Stephen: Mummy, I have special classes tomorrow morning so I will have to leave early.

Mummy: Special classes are often conducted after college hours right?

Stephen: Sir is having other plans tomorrow evening and so he said he will take the class early in the morning just before the college starts.

Mummy: Really? (*sigh*) Ok, so what time do you have to leave?

Stephen: At about 6:15 A.M.; I will get on the 1st bus. It arrives at the stop at around 6:20 A.M.

I was so eager to chat with her that I hardly could sleep that night. Expectations were high, and I was eager and tensed at the same time.

I hopped on to the 1st bus as planned. It was still quite dark and there was hardly anyone on that bus except for a few guys in front. Getting down at Manorama Junction would mean that I would have to walk to my college after the chat session with Rachel as I would not have enough money to get back home if I were to take another bus from there to my college. I would also have to pay about 10 rupees to the internet café;

10 rupees for 1 hour was expensive compared to the one located near my home, but at that time all these things did not matter. I was ready to walk to college; I would do anything for her.

It was an hour's journey to this place called Manorama Junction.

The bus was speeding and the cold air was gushing on my face and I was already dreaming with my eyes closed—of holding her hand, getting married to her, kissing her, making love to her, and whatnot. Suddenly, I felt someone sitting next to me, and then I felt him touching my thighs as though unknowingly. I was feeling very uncomfortable; it was the bus conductor. His hands went further above my thighs until his hand was touching my trouser zipper. I was shocked, I was being molested by an idiot. I could see the fire in his eyes. Rachel was off my mind that moment, my dreams were interrupted, not knowing how to react to that situation I jumped up and stood the rest of my journey shocked about what had happened. Not being able to process or react.

I got down at the stop almost in tears not knowing whom to tell about what had happened on that bus, but then I told myself that it was fine and that nothing had happened. All this pain would not go in vain; for now, the focus was on Rachel–she was waiting. I rushed to the main entrance of the internet café only to see that it was closed; actually, I had reached early and there was still about 10 minutes for the café to open. I waited patiently, consoling myself, holding back my tears as there was a battle being fought within me which could not be explained. There was fear and agony within me.

Rachel was online...

Stephen: Hi

Rachel: Hi, where had you been? I need to get to bed... I am tired.

Stephen: You alright?

Rachel: What the fuck, what did you want to tell me?

Stephen: Why are you getting angry?

Rachel: Fuck you, Stephen, I don't have time for this.

Stephen: Why are you abusing? Just calm down...

Rachel: I don't owe you anything you asshole; just fuck off. I don't have time for this...

Rachel offline...

I was broken and in tears as I walked slowly to my college. People change; some change a lot but I still loved her. She was my everything.

Chapter 6

It was the first period, the teacher had not yet arrived, the class was noisy as usual like in any other college; that was the first time I saw her, Caren.

Stephen: Who is that?

Shinoy: She is the new girl I was talking about Chetai (brother in Malayalam).

Shinoy was my cousin brother and we both were doing our graduation together.

Stephen: We are almost midterm then how did she get admission?

Shinoy: Not sure but she is hot. There is a guy with her, maybe her brother.

Stephen: Hmm...

She walked into the classroom and there was a sudden silence. She was wearing a velvet purple-colored salwar top. She broke all definitions in my mind of a perfect woman. She was beautiful, very beautiful.

Shinoy: Hi...what is your name? (in Malayalam)

Caren: Caren! What is yours? And who is that guy (indicating Chetai)? (Caren answered back in English)

Shinoy: Enda? ("What?" in Malayalam) Don't you know Malayalam?

Caren: Speak in English if you want to speak to me...

Shinoy was angry and felt insulted. He told me what had happened. Shinoy and his friends were not good at conversing in English, so they wanted me to speak to her in English–to basically snub her and I took up the gory task.

Stephen: Hi!

Caren: Hi... What is your name?

Stephen: What is yours?

Caren: I am Caren (*grinning*)

She extended her hand to shake hands.

Stephen: Stephen! (*shaking her hand. Her hands were warm and sweaty. I could feel her hand shivering, but her confidence was spot on. She smelled like a rose; the smell of her perspiration mixed with her rose perfume made the situation even sweeter.*)

Stephen: You are very pretty.

Caren: I know (*smiling*) You look good too...

Stephen: Really?

Caren: Yes. I saw you scanning me when I walked in. (*grinning*)

Shinoy and friends were watching us speak from a distance.

Stephen: I really like you.

Caren: (*smiling*) Me too.

Stephen: Excuse me?

Caren: Yeah... Me too. (*laughing out loud*)

Suddenly heard a voice from behind. "Caren!"

It was her cousin?

Caren: Hey, nice meeting you. (*smile*) Talk to you later, bye.

Stephen: Yeah, bye.

After Caren exited the scene Shinoy and his friends rushed towards me.

Shinoy: Chetai, what happened? What did she say?

Stephen: I told her that I liked her. (*grinning*)

I was all confused. I just wanted to amuse her but I did not expect her to reply to me like that. I did not want to share my thoughts about the whole conversation with Shinoy and friends.

Shinoy: Chetai! And what did she say?

Stephen: She said she likes me as well. (*still grinning*)

Shinoy: Oh my God! You are a stud, Chetai.

All his friends were praising me and making me a star among themselves yet again, while I was only thinking of her boldness and the answers she gave me to my questions. I was suddenly feeling cold. I could feel the Kochi breeze on my face and I had all goosebumps on my hands. I suddenly looked for her around. She was at a distance with Robin. She was looking at me and the moment she saw me looking at her she turned her face to Robin. After a few seconds, her eyes again looked in the direction where I was standing with the guys. I was still staring at her and this time she smiled. She was blushing. She was very beautiful. Her tan complexion made her look even sexier; her eyes spoke a lot.

That night was beautiful. It made me feel better, it made me feel better after Rachel's abuses as I never e-mailed or messaged her after that but I could not forget her. She was all stuck to my heart, but I liked this new change. It was beautiful. Caren was beautiful and I loved the smell of her perspiration. The fresh smell of sweat from a woman turned me on always.

Chapter 7

I was sitting and studying for my exams—final year exams and then graduation would be over. I looked at the phone (landline phone) on my table. Daddy and Mummy were watching TV in the sitting room while I was in my bedroom, so it was safe to call Caren. I wanted to get married to her, but Robin? Robin was always with her—protecting her. They both always walked as a couple. I have seen her buy cigarettes for him, I have seen her eating with him, I have seen her with him always. It looked as if they were not cousins, rather best friends. They never looked like friends to me but hey, can't a girl and boy be just good friends?

I decided to call Caren. I wanted to know if I could send my parents to her place and if her parents would be ready to give her in marriage to me even though I was not ready for marriage I just wanted to let her know how committed I was in this relationship. I wanted to live my life with her and so I decided to call her, to ask her one last time. She had told me many times earlier that Robin was only a friend and nothing else to her but this time I wanted to let her know that I was serious about her and hence decided to call her.

Her phone was ringing...

Caren: Hello...

Stephen: Hi

Caren: Hey, Stephen. How are you? Have you finished studying?

Stephen: Almost ready for next weeks exam

Caren: So what plans after graduation?

Stephen: My brother-in-law and my sister are in Dubai, so most probably will go get a job in Dubai if they take me.

Caren: How about post-graduation?

Stephen: Not now... Not in the mood to study anything more at this time. I have to go to do some work, need to help Daddy.

Caren: Why, what happened?

Stephen: No nothing... He needs to rest a little as well, isn't it?

Caren: But the business is going on well, right? And your Daddy is not very old either. Why don't you join your Daddy's business?

Stephen: I am not very interested in that. I prefer working somewhere; moreover, it is not my business, it is my Daddy's and my brother-in-law's.

Caren: Oh, come on! Your Daddy's is yours, right?

Stephen: It is not like that, Caren, it is complicated. I would prefer working for someone else first and then if everything works well then I would not mind joining the family business. I want to be able to invest money into the business first and then join it.

Caren: Oh, that's great! Good... So your life is kind of set. Lucky you, I am not sure what I am going to do after graduation.

Stephen: Why don't you do your post-graduation?

Caren: Na... Not in the mood, same as you. I want to relax for some time after the exams and then I will decide what to do depending on my mood and situation. So what else Stephen?

Stephen: I called to ask you something.

Caren: Yeah, shoot. (*chuckles*)

Stephen: I want to know the truth, what is your relationship with Robin?

Caren: We have discussed this so many times, Stephen; we are good friends and nothing else.

Stephen: Are you sure, because I see you both always together and you look more than friends. In fact, you both look like a couple.

Caren: Gosh (*laugh out loud*) Couple? No way, we are very close friends. We are neighbors and we are together from school days and that's it. I never thought you would think of us like that, ever; unlike the others, I always felt that you were broad-minded.

Stephen: Hey, don't take it otherwise. I was only asking.

Caren: Can't a boy and girl be just friends? I don't understand this world.

Stephen: Relax... Cool... I was only asking. Anyway, let's leave that topic.

With all my confidence I was going to open up to her.

Stephen: Actually, I called to tell you something important.

Caren: Yeah, go on. I am listening...

Stephen: I like you a lot and would want to get married to you. Well, do you love me?

Caren: Yeah... I don't mind getting married to you. You are a nice guy and I like you as well.

Stephen: Then shall I send my parents to your place to speak to your parents?

Caren: Are you crazy? We are only doing our graduation now. Don't you think it is too early?

Stephen: I know, but I just want our parents to know about this and then later after a year or two we could get married. Obviously, your parents would be concerned about what I am going to do in the future. I will be going to Dubai to pursue a career out there, and I am sure we could convince your parents.

Caren: I don't know. I am kind of confused. Are you serious, Stephen?

Stephen: Of course, yes, I am very much serious.

Caren: I am not sure how my parents are going to take it, I am very nervous.

Stephen: Just relax! We will wait until our exams are over and then I will come with my parents to your place and I am sure we can convince your parents.

Caren: No, Stephen, is this necessary?

Stephen: Just leave everything to me. I will handle this without any casualties (*chuckles*) Don't worry. Ok, bye. Study for now.

Caren: Yeah, bye.

I disconnected the phone and was thinking of a way to tell about all this to my Mummy and Daddy when suddenly the phone bell rang.

Stephen: Hello!

Other side: What the fuck do you think of yourself?

Stephen: Hello! (*shocked*) Who is this?

Other side: Fucker! Don't you know who I am?

Stephen: Can you stop abusing and let me know who you are and what do you want?

Other side: I am Robin, Caren's boyfriend.

Stephen: Robin! Boyfriend? But Caren said you were friends.

Robin: We both love each other, and our parents know about all this, so please keep away from her. I don't want you to unnecessarily disturb her anymore.

Stephen: Robin... I did ask her several times about you and her before proposing to her.

Robin: now I am telling you... Just leave us both alone, and don't call her ever again (*hung up the phone*).

Why did such things always have to happen to me? Why me? I asked her so many times if she liked him then why didn't she tell me?

Caren might have given my phone number to Robin else how would he know my number? Should I call back and ask? Why should I call her anymore, to tell her what? She was just using me for her entertainment. I was a fool and will remain a fool. I am not quite handsome either.

I cried that night. I pulled out my old album again. *Rachel! Maybe God has bigger plans for me*, I told myself. What if all this is for the good but why did Caren have to lie? Why all this drama?

I had a high temperature the following day. I was being monitored by my parents; the temperature was so high and my situation worsened to an extent that I was unconscious... blabbering about Rachel.

My parents saw the album below my pillow and decided to burn all of Rachel's photographs as they thought that it was all because of her thoughts that my condition was worsening.

All of Rachel's photographs were set on fire while I stayed unconscious in bed. All my memories were turned into ashes within minutes while my heart ached in solitude.

Chapter 8

Where on one side the college ended, Daddy's business was not doing well. I was waiting to get myself placed in Dubai. That evening my parents came and asked me if I liked Ann. She was our family friend's daughter and we were all very close to each other but I had never looked at her in that sense.

Daddy: If you like her then we can speak to her parents.

Stephen: I don't know... I have not looked at her in that sense.

Daddy: Then why don't you start looking at her in that sense from now on? (*smiling*) We will go to her place tomorrow.

Stephen: Yeah ok.

"What would you like to have, tea or coffee?" asked Annamma Aunty, Ann's mother, and before I could reply Ann said—

Ann: He likes coffee Maa... (*looking at me smiling*)

Ann brought coffee after a while for all of us, with some marble cake. Everyone was talking to each other and I was only looking at her, trying to analyze her body structure.

She had naturally brown hair and she was extremely fair. She was quite pretty and was very smart, a go-getter, she loved driving cars. She was more of a guy within than a girl.

She saw me looking at her, checking her out and she nodded her head in a gesture asking me "what?" and I shook my head back in return which meant "nothing". We both smiled at each other and made eye contact several times that evening.

She was a very sweet girl but I still could not digest the fact that I might have to get married to her? I thought to myself that I better give it some time. I loved Rachel and maybe I was afraid from within of another rejection, but I always knew that everything happened for a reason and if this relationship did not work out it would be for the better like the rest.

Daddy's business was not at all in a good shape and my brother-in-law who also happens to be the partner was also least bothered about all that was happening with this business. Daddy was selling all the property, land, and other assets one after the other to save his drowning business. On the other hand, the other partner only watched all this happen and did nothing to help from his end. At last, we only had our house left to sell and that is when I told my Daddy to stop. I told him to wind up or to sell the business along with its goodwill and to end this partnership as soon as possible.

Daddy: How will we live if we stop this business? What will we eat?

Stephen: I will take care of you and Mummy, don't worry, trust me. I will not let this house go away from your hands Daddy.

Soon our business was bought by another company and I started working for a small software company in Kochi as a call center executive. Shinoy had arranged that job for me. The only problem was that I was only being paid about 13,000 rupees and I needed at least 28,000 rupees a month to settle the various installments from private finance companies and banks from whom my Daddy had taken money as loans to run the business. I understood the fact that no financial help was going to come from overseas and the so-called partner would not do anything to help us. My Daddy lost everything which he had made all his life and I was helpless, could not even yell at the partner because the partner happened to be my sister's husband. I cared more about my sister's life than ours which was almost over.

I tried to contact all my relatives abroad whom my Daddy had helped in some way or the other when they were in need, but all of them kept avoiding me and my pleas. Some of them would not pick up my call. I contacted a few of my Daddy's friends as well, but no one replied positively. Daddy would not call anyone for help as he was still in shock that everything was over. I understood his situation. He was like a king who had lost his kingdom and pride.

I then decided to send an e-mail to my brother-in-law. I literally begged him in that e-mail to take me to Dubai. He replied to my e-mail saying that I was only a graduate and I had no experience or the skills for the gulf market. He literally made me feel worthless and useless for the gulf. I pleaded with him because I knew that I would never get a job in India that could pay me 30,000 rupees a month and the only way to get that was to head to Dubai, to the gulf.

Then one day I received an e-mail from my brother-in-law, it was my visa on arrival confirmation. I was going to Dubai.

Chapter 9

Dubai was not as expected. It was tough, but I found a job for myself. I sent almost 95% of my salary home so that Daddy could sort out things back in India. I stayed with my brother-in-law and sister. I paid a part of the remaining 5% of my salary to my brother-in-law as my share for living at their place and eating the food which they had prepared.

I was insulted by my brother-in-law always and my sister had to literally fight with her husband to defend me. One-night things got out of hand and I decided to leave. For the sake of my sister's life, I wanted her at least to live peacefully with her family instead of defending and fighting for me.

I called Hassan Ikka (*"Ikka" means big brother in Malayalam*); he was my colleague.

Hassan Ikka was going to Kerala the next day for a month on vacation along with his family and so he recommended that I could stay at his place until I found another place for myself. With 20 dirhams in my pocket, I left my brother-in-law's home that night and stayed at Hassan Ikka's abode. The very next day by God's grace Hassan Ikka was able to find a place for me to stay. I had to stay with a couple, they had a small room in their apartment which they wanted to rent out. I did not have to pay any advance, and luckily enough they agreed that I could pay when I received my salary.

Things were getting difficult. My expenses were increasing and that meant that I would not be able to send home money as much as I used to. I tried out ways to cut down on my expenses to the extent of staying hungry and stealing drinking water from the house owner couple.

After work, one day while getting down the tower where our office was located, Hassan Ikka said–

Hassan Ikka: What are your plans for the weekend?

Stephen: Nothing, have some clothes to wash and that's it.

Hassan Ikka: Come home if you are free on Friday night.

Stephen: Will try!

Hassan Ikka: Enjoy your weekend, bye.

Stephen: Good night.

I was rushing to cross the busy road. It was the weekend and so there was more traffic than usual. All the cars were moving at an ant's speed; suddenly, I saw a familiar face. It was Clara, the sister of one of our family friend. It had been many years that her entire family shifted to Dubai. This was a surprise and she recognized me. She asked me to get in her car but I hesitated, moreover I was all drenched in sweat because of the heat and humidity outside, and she looked very rich—driving a fancy car. I did not want to get inside her car and create an awkward situation; however, she understood that I was kind of shocked seeing her all of a sudden, and she was shocked as well. She hurriedly pulled out her business card and handed it over to me and said "call me when you can... Today itself if possible" and she smiled. Her car passed by and was lost in the weekend traffic of Dubai.

Later that night after reaching home I called Clara.

Clara: Hello!

Stephen: Hi... It's me, Stephen.

Clara: What a surprise (*laughing*) How are you, my dear?

Stephen: I am good, going on.

Clara: How is Uncle and Aunty?

Stephen: All are well by God's Grace.

Clara: How long have you been here in Dubai?

Stephen: 6 months, almost.

Clara: Hey, wait! Let me call you back. (*phone disconnected*)

Clara knew the difficulties and expenses of a fresh expat in Dubai so she called me back. Our conversation lasted for about 2 hours until my mobile battery was completely drained. I told her everything that had happened–the reason for me coming to Dubai, the way I got out of my brother-in-law's house, everything. I felt so relieved after a long time. I felt as though I had become light from within. Someone was ready to listen to me. Before disconnecting the call she asked me to be ready the next day. She wanted to take me out for lunch. I told her that I had to get back to Hassan Ikka's house in the evening. She promised to drop me at his place as well.

Chapter 10

It was a hot day. I slept a little longer than usual. I felt much better and happier today. I got dressed for my lunch with Clara.

Clara called me at about 11:00 A.M. to ask about my location and she said that she would come to pick me up at 12:30 P.M.

Lunch on a weekend meant luxury—good quality and quantity of food were rare and a blessing; I was very much looking forward to my free lunch.

It was 12:30 P.M. and in a few minutes, my mobile rang.

Clara: Hi, I am below your building near the parking in a white Mercedez.

Stephen: I will come downstairs in a moment.

Clara: Ok. (*phone disconnected*)

She was waiting in her car downstairs but this time it was a different car. *Well, how many cars does she own,* I wondered! She might be filthy rich I told myself.

Clara: Hi! Get in. (*smiling*) How are you?

Stephen: I am good and you?

Clara: Good... going on. Shall we have a drink before we have lunch... like an appetizer? You drink, right?

Stephen: Sure... Yeah, occasionally.

We walked into this posh hotel and we went to the bar first.

Clara: There is a very nice restaurant here; we will eat lunch there. So what would you like to have?

Stephen: Beer would be fine.

Clara: Ok... (*looking at the bartender: 2 pints of Heineken*)

Bartender: Sure, Ma'am. Would you like some sides to go with it?

Clara: Chicken lollipops and roasted peanuts.

Bartender: Perfect, Ma'am, you can make yourself comfortable. (*pointing at a table in the corner of the hall*) We will serve you at the table.

Clara: Thank you! Are you comfortable, Stephen, or do you want to sit somewhere else?

Stephen: No, this is fine.

Clara: So... Tell me...

Stephen: I told you almost everything (*smile*) You tell me about yourself.

Clara: What to say about myself (*sigh*) I was married but things did not work out so got divorced. I have a daughter, her name is Zoyie and she is 5 years old.

Stephen: Why did you get divorced?

Clara: It's complicated.

Stephen: I am listening... Don't tell me if you are not comfortable.

Clara: No... It is not that, not sure where to start. Hmm... It was an arranged marriage. Mathew is well-educated and was well-off financially. His whole family is here in Dubai. Everything was fine in the beginning but as months passed by Mathew was beginning to be more and more possessive. I work for the *Desert Times* Magazine here, in the marketing wing; and you know how marketing is right. I will have to carry myself in classy clothes, I might have to make calls, many calls would be coming in for me, some of them could be men; in fact, most of them would be men from different nationalities and he would just start acting weird. He never wanted me to give up my job because he liked the money as I was contributing to our expenses. He used to literally hit me at times if I was late to get home. Sometimes I will have to wait and complete a meeting before I call it a day and get back home.

Stephen: Hmm

Clara: He used to literally rape me in bed at times. (*silence, trying to pull back her tears*) He used to literally abuse me (almost crying)

Stephen: Hey, relax... Please don't cry. (*silence*)

Clara: No, I am fine. (*wiping her tears with tissue from the tissue holder on the table*) I was a good wife, I took care of his parents, I was available for him always. I also contributed towards his business by taking a loan against my salary, I did everything a wife should be doing but I had to make a decision one night when he literally made me bleed after his madness.

The bartender had brought our order.

Stephen: Thank you. (*smile*)

Bartender exits...

Clara: I hated sleeping with him. He used to rape me calling out the names of other women. He used to arrange parties at our home and he used to literally make ways for his friends to look at me and then when they were gone he used to yell at me saying that it was all my fault and that I was a bitch, a slut and what not.

Stephen: like how?

Clara: For instance, if there is a party he will say that I should look very nice, elegant, classy and then he would suggest a dress for me to wear, mostly revealing low neck dresses; and then when his friends come in he would ask me to sit with them and drink, now what am I supposed to do? Cut off my boobs and my bum? Men will look... I have a kid and my breasts would look bigger than usual as I was still breastfeeding my child. First of all, why does he want me to sit with them? He never liked me asking him such questions. If I ask him "why?" then he would say "are you trying to insult me in front of my friends?" and then if I said I won't wear a particular dress, he will start saying "oh, so you want to look like a Behan Ji (village girl/elderly, uneducated woman) in front of my friends!" and then after all the arguments or a fight he used to literally bang me like an asshole, taking all his anger on me; he used to literally tear me apart. He enjoyed hurting me, he smiled and laughed while he fucked me like an animal. He was crazy, mad.

I was in shock after hearing all this. More than her situation, I was shocked because she told me everything, too much detail. *Who would treat such a beautiful and classy woman like that*, I wondered.

Clara had changed a lot from what she was. I knew her from a very small age, from the time we stayed in Calcutta now called Kolkata, our families used to meet up at each other's place, her flat used to be in a very tall building. She was on some 8th floor, she was the one who taught me the names of cars. I used to sit on her lap in her balcony and we used to identify each car that passed by below on the road. She is almost 10 years elder. We always sat together whenever we met.

I loved sitting on her lap. I loved her smell. I loved the smell of her sweat. I still remember telling everyone that she was my girlfriend. I think those were my first erotic experiences in life. Little did I know what that feeling was but I knew that something was different. The press of her breasts on my back, while I sat on her lap, felt good. She was my first love, ever. I always felt protected when I was with her, I always felt respected when I was around her. She was the most dynamic and smartest woman I had ever known, and here she sat today in front of me. Maybe it was destiny that we had to meet again. I felt as though I was being pampered once again. I felt safe again.

Clara: You want another drink?

Stephen: No, I am ok.

Clara: Then shall we go to the restaurant and eat?

Stephen: Yes, ok

Clara indicated the bartender for her bill and after she had paid the bill we proceeded to the restaurant of that hotel.

Clara: What would you like to have sweetheart? (*smiling at me*)

From the time we had known each other she always addressed me as sweetheart, love, darling but calling me "sweetheart" at this age? It felt kind of odd.

Stephen: Anything...Whatever you are ordering.

Clara: Just order whatever you like.

I looked at the menu and decided to go with the North Indian Thali

Stephen: I would like to have a North Indian Thali.

Clara indicated and a bearer came to our table to take the order

Clara: He will have North Indian Thali and I would like to have mixed fried rice and Chilly Chicken, mildly spicy, and a bottle of water

Bearer: Sure, madam. Do you want the water cold or room temperature?

Clara: Cold.

Bearer: Sure. Anything else madam?

Clara: Bring this for now and we will let you know if we want anything more.

Bearer: Very well madam.

Food was brought to our table, everything looked extra classy. The bearer poured water in our glasses and left the premises.

Clara: So let's attack. (*laughing*) Hey, what do you have on your plate?

Stephen: chapattis, chicken tikka, mutton curry, daal tadka, aloo muttar (dry), some cauliflower sabji and a portion of white basmati long grain rice.

Clara: Looks great! Let's eat.

While eating we shared our food with each other; as usual, we bonded so well even after so many years. She ordered some rasmalai as dessert for both of us.

She knew that I loved Indian sweets. The meal was quite heavy, and I wanted to take a nap. That was a decent meal I had had in months I could say. The food tasted extra tasty.

Clara: Shall we go home? Everyone would be happy to see you.

Stephen: Sure!

Clara took me to her apartment, it was a huge 4-bedroom apartment. Everyone was surprisingly happy to see me. We all talked for a while Zoyie liked me a lot. She loved showing me her toys. I understood that everyone wanted to take a nap; usually, Friday afternoons, especially during the summer are meant for sleeping in the UAE for many, and so I slowly went to Clara and told her to take me home.

Clara: Where are you going? I will drop you at your colleague's place in the evening don't worry, for now, you take a nap. Come I will show you a place.

And she pulled my hands and took me to her room. Apart from the big king-sized bed where she and her daughter slept there was another sofa bed. She opened up the sofa bed and asked me to sleep on that. After putting her daughter to sleep on their bed she went into her attached washroom to change. After a while, she came out wearing a t-shirt and cycling shorts. I could not take my eyes off her beautiful thick thighs, her knees and skin were glowing like silk. She asked me if I wanted to use her toilet, and so I went in and washed my face and hands. I looked around for a towel, and I took the towel which was on the rail, and something was there under the towel. It was Clara's bra and panties. I quickly took them in my hands. The bra was padded and wired, made of black lace and her panties were of the same material as well, it smelt of her perfume and sweat. The smell was quite familiar. I knew that smell since childhood, and they looked so pretty. I quickly kept it back and started wiping my face with the towel when I heard a knock on the door. It was from Clara.

Clara: Do you need a towel sweetheart?

Stephen: No... I am good. (*I quickly came out of the washroom*) I used the one in here.

Clara's face flushed.

Clara: That was my towel. (*blushing*)

Stephen: That's ok.

Clara was still blushing and came close to my ear and said "*sorry!*" and I looked at her and whispered back (*smiling*) "*it's ok...*"

She pulled my hands, took me to the sofa bed, and asked me to sleep after which she went back to her bed to lie down with Zoyie.

I could see her and Zoyie from where I was sleeping. Clara was very beautiful, tan-skinned. This was the first time I was seeing her as an adult. I could clearly see her perky nipples. She was not wearing her bra and her hands and legs were so silky and clean, well-maintained. She had beautiful nails and her hair was so silky and thick. I could literally feel my body temperature rising. Clara opened her beautiful eyes and looked at me. She saw me staring at her. She whispered (in an intention not to wake her daughter) "*sleep*" (*smiling*). I closed my eyes and slept for some time peacefully.

After a few hours in the evening...

Clara: Hey, sweets! Wake up. (*coffee mug in her hand*) Have some coffee.

Stephen: Thanks!

Clara: I will drop you in a while.

Stephen: Sure, thanks.

After drinking the coffee, I went back into the washroom to wash my face and mouth. This time the bra and panties were missing. She was wearing them; might have worn them back after her nap. I used her towel to wipe my face as earlier. I was all set and ready to go and attend Hassan Ikka's party.

Clara brought in a big plastic bag full of eatables and snacks—chips, cookies etc.

Clara: This is all for you. And this is my personal mobile number, call me whenever you need me. You just have to give me a missed call and I will call you back, you can SMS me as well. If I am busy I might take some time to respond, so please relax if you don't hear back from me immediately.

Stephen: Yeah, thanks; but what will I do with so much of things?

Clara: Nothing in that will get spoilt any time soon. So snack in the evenings my dear, and don't worry we will first go to your place, leave this bag there and then I will drop you wherever you want to. Ok?

Stephen: Ah...thanks!

Clara: I will get dressed in a moment and then we will go. On the way back home she was all pepped up and happy. The music was loud in the car and Zoyie was happy and yelling in the back seat.

Clara: Have not seen Zoyie this happy in a long time, she likes you a lot. (*blushing*)

The car was parked exactly from where I was picked up in the afternoon.

Clara: Do you need help to carry the bag to your room?

Stephen: Nope... I can manage.

Clara: Ok, we will wait here. Come fast, ok!

After a while, I was back and she took me to Hassan Ikka's place as promised and on reaching there Zoyie wished me good night and Clara gave me a quick hug.

Clara: Bye, sweetheart, call me ok. (smiling)

I knocked at the door of Hassan Ikka's apartment and the door opened and Hassan Ikka welcomed me.

Stephen: How are you Ikka?

Hassan: Alhamdullillah...

And he introduced me to his friends and family, the whole place was smelling of rich mutton biriyani.

It was a nice day—a day full of good food and good vibes. While walking back to my flat that night I felt very happy. Something that I had not felt in months.

Clara was beautiful. She was very kind and I liked her company. I liked her vibe–positiveness and above all, I felt safe with her. The inner child in me wanted to be with her always.

Chapter 11

It was more than a year in UAE and I was looking out for another job, not because I did not like the current job but because I wanted to get a better salary; for better salary meant being able to handle the issues back home in a better and faster way and at the same time being able to increase my standard of living here in the UAE and being able to save some money to go back home for the holidays. Clara was already helping me out to get a better job. She was also telling her friends about me and was circulating my resume as well. She even managed to get me an interview at her office but due to lack of experience, I was never offered that job.

At last, I got a job with the Sharjah Government. Back at home, everyone was glad that I was going to get a better salary, but Clara was the happiest. She was happy that I was becoming successful. She was happy in seeing me happy.

Clara... I call her Clara now but when I was a kid I always used to call her Clara Chechi (*sister in Malayalam*); for some reason, I did not want to call her Chechi again. She had become more than just a Chechi to me now. She was my best friend, in fact, more than a friend. There was nothing that Clara did not know about me and there was nothing that I never knew about Clara. We shared a rare bond.

I had called home to tell about the happy news about my new job, and that is when Daddy told me something.

Daddy: I spoke to John, Ann's father yesterday, he said that they are not interested in a relationship with us.

Stephen: What! did you speak to Ann?

Daddy: They said that it was a collective decision of the family. They did not want to get their daughter married into a sinking ship.

Stephen: It is ok, Daddy. What else? How is everyone else?

Daddy: All are fine here. All this is happening because of me, right? You both liked each other, isn't it?

Stephen: Leave all that. I got a new job; now things will get better.

Mummy: Helloo, Son... Don't worry you will get someone better than her; you don't worry. (*silence*)

My parents knew that I was holding back my tears and I was pretending to be happy as though nothing had happened.

Stephen: I am ok, Mummy. Everything will get better; as long as you and Daddy are happy I am happy. Don't worry about me.

Mummy: When are you coming home?

Stephen: I will come soon, Mummy, I will come soon. Where is Daddy?

Daddy: The phone is on speaker, I can hear you, don't worry. What else can I say...

Stephen: I am ok Daddy, you both relax. I am fine. Shall I keep the phone?

Daddy: Ok, bye! (*phone disconnected*).

I could not stop crying. I cried like a baby. I felt so embarrassed, I felt ashamed. Everyone so far had rejected me. No one liked me. I decide to send an e-mail to Ann...

e-mail to Ann

Dear Ann,

My Daddy told me that you guys had rejected my proposal. Didn't you have any feelings for me? What happened? I just got a new job now with the Sharjah Government. I will be able to sort out everything sooner now. Just give me some more time. I thought you would understand but you've proved me wrong.

Please reply.

Bye!

After a few hours, I received a reply.

Reply from Ann

Dear Stephen,

Can we talk? Can you call me, if possible?

Bye.

I did not have enough cash to buy a phone card and so I called Clara. I told her what had happened

Clara: Call Ann immediately and speak to her and don't worry, everything will be fine. Please don't cry anymore, especially when you are speaking to Ann, keep your cool I will send you the phone recharge number in 5 minutes.

She immediately bought a phone card and I got my phone balance recharged. I took a deep breath and called Ann.

Phone bell ringing...

Ann: Hello!

Stephen: Hi!

Ann: Oh hi...

Stephen: Yeah, why did you ask me to call you?

Ann: Stephen, don't get me wrong but I had no other choice. It was a collective decision; I could not say "no!"

Stephen: Do you love me. I mean did you ever have feelings for me?

Ann: yes, I love you but I will not do anything against my parents' will. I will obey whatever decision they take on my behalf.

Stephen: Good, that is what a good and obedient daughter should do. Don't worry, I am not angry with you or anything.

Ann: I am sorry!

Stephen: It's ok. You take care of yourself and be happy always. Bye.

Ann: Bye.

(disconnected the phone)

I could not bear the rejection. I cried and pulled Rachel's picture out of my purse and cried even more like a baby, holding the picture close to my chest *(my phone started ringing...it was Clara)*

Clara: Hello, did you call her?

Stephen: Hi... (*silence*)

Clara: Are you crying? What happened?

Stephen: I am fine... I am alright!

Clara: Yeah, I can understand you are alright. What did she say?

Stephen: She said she loved me but will not do anything against her parents' will.

Clara: Fuckin bitch! Let her go, man. She does not deserve a person like you. She does not know what she is losing, you relax. I will come and pick you up in the evening.

Stephen: No it's fine. I just want to be alone for some time.

Clara: I said I will come and pick you up in the evening, not now. You have all the time until then to be alone. (*silence for a few seconds*) Don't cry anymore. I will pick you up in the evening. We will have dinner together, ok?

Stephen: hmm

Clara: Ok bye, and stop sulking. See you in the evening.

Stephen: Yeah. Ok, bye.

In the evening Clara picked me up and we went to this bar. As usual, we had beer and we did not speak much that evening. She wanted to leave me at peace as well so never spoke or asked me anything. She knew I was very upset and was trying to cheer me up, diverting my mind. We ate a little and then left the premises...

Clara: Shall I drop you at your place?

Stephen: No... Can you take me for a drive? Or better you drive back home and from there I will take a sharing taxi or something and get back to my accommodation

Clara: hmm... Ok. By the way, how is your new accommodation?

Stephen: There are 3 bedrooms and 2 guys each in each room. It is a nice place, all bachelors, all from different companies. It's good, nice guys.

Clara took me for a drive and then drove back to her place. On the way to her place, there was not much of speaking. The music was on and tears were flowing from my eyes. Suddenly, I felt her hands on my hands. She was patting my hand indicating that everything would be fine and to relax. Her car stopped below her building. It was quite late in the night already and her parking lot was very dark. She parked her car and then turned to me.

Clara: You are very handsome and you are a gem of a person, let those losers just fuck off. You just concentrate on your work now and everything will be fine. It is not your loss that they rejected your proposal, in fact, it is their loss.

Stephen: Why does this happen always to me? (*I could not hold back my tears anymore and burst out into tears*)

Clara just hugged me and put my head to her chest and comforted me.

Clara: Crying is good at times. Cry as much as you want, let all that pain flow out.

I was crying like a child. My tears were wetting her white blouse. She patted my back. She ran her fingers through my hair trying to console me, then she lifted my head up with her hands and wiped my tears, and kissed me on my cheeks, and then on my lips. I was shocked at first at her gesture. There was this terrible silence all of a sudden, but I felt so much better and stopped crying. I went forward slowly and kissed Clara on her lips, her eyes closed slowly, her soft and puffy lips were sucking my lower lip, I could feel her saliva in my mouth. Her lips were warm, her hands were on my cheeks and we kept smooching each other while my whole body trembled, and I was shivering. I started kissing her neck and then I went further down. She understood that I wanted to kiss her breasts and so she opened a couple of her buttons from her blouse for me. I could see her black lace bra and her beautiful deep cleavage. I kissed those beautiful bulges and then went back to kissing her lips. There was an urgency within me and while kissing her lips my hands were groping her beautiful breasts, trying to pull out her breast from inside her bra. Her bra was quite tight and so it was difficult. She was trying to help me out. With one of her hands, she was trying to pull out her breast; she did not want the kissing to stop so she slowly opened a couple of more buttons by herself and took my hands and placed it on her breasts. She looked into my eyes and I stopped kissing her and went down to kiss her breasts again. I slowly put my hands into one of the padded cups of her bra. I could feel her nipples on my palm. She quickly monitored the surroundings to see if anyone was watching while I pulled out one of her breasts from inside her bra; I then gently kissed that beautiful black and rubbery nipples while she pressed my head with her hands thrusting my face on her breasts. I sucked and kissed her nipples. Her nipples were wet with my saliva, she moaned as I was sucking her nipples hard. I was so hungry for her other breast that I was trying to pull down her other cup but it was tight, alternatively, I tried to lift up her bra. There was a sense of urgency within both of us now. We both were breathing heavily and sweating. I just wanted to make love to her right there in the car, but with the limited space in her car, things were getting difficult. I was still trying to pull out her other breast when suddenly her phone started ringing. It was from her flat. She pushed me and indicated me to remain silent. She picked up her phone. She was still breathing fast.

Clara: Hello.

Zoyie: Maa...why are you not coming upstairs?

Clara: Maa is coming baby. Who else is at home?

Zoyie: Only grandpa is here with me. The rest have all gone out for dinner.

Clara: Maa will come up in 5 minutes sweetheart. (*phone disconnected*)

I went back to kissing her lips and she not wanting to resist said in a low voice. "I have to go... please." I kept kissing her. She started to put back her buttons when I went back to suck her beautiful nipple once again and she moaned and said "please I have to go!" I was not listening to her and I started squeezing her soft breast. It was so soft and silky, and then she pushed me off slowly. I again bent down to suck her nipple when she held my face with her hands and kissed my lips tight and said firmly this time but in a soft tone, "Stop! I need to go... please, my baby is waiting for me." She quickly put back her breast into her bra, adjusted the support elastics, corrected her bra wires to set her breasts in position. I watched her button her blouse and set her hair with her fingers. She quickly pulled down her car sunshade flap which had a mirror beneath it with lights. She hurriedly checked her lipstick and her face and then put back the flap in position and told me. "*Let's get out!*" She indicated that she gets out of the car first and check if her father or daughter was watching from the balcony. The plan was that if they were watching she would just get out of the car take her things and walk to her apartment while I sneaked out after a few minutes. She said she would later lock her car using her remote control locking system from her balcony. So she stepped out of her car slowly and looked up at the balcony. The balcony was empty. She sighed in relief and indicated that I get out of the car fast. I dropped her at the main entrance of her apartment and hurriedly hugged her. She smiled at me and said, "*don't cry anymore*" and I whispered in her ear "*sorry!*"

"No… It was not supposed to happen. This is the first time I have touched another man after my wedding other than my husband. Let it be our little secret; and let's not do it ever again. I am no good for you my dear. It was good as long as it lasted and that's it! Ok? Good night, bye. Now, go fast," Clara replied.

I could not sleep that night and I could not believe what had just happened. It was my first encounter with a woman. I had never touched a woman ever in my life before. I was constantly dreaming of making love to Clara, and I just could not hold back myself. I looked around my room and my roommate was fast asleep. I decided to call Clara. It was already 1:00 A.M., and so I decided to send her an SMS.

Stephen: I can't sleep.

Almost immediately I received a reply.

Clara: I am awake as well!

Stephen: All ok there right!

Clara: Yeah… All well.

Stephen: Today was the best day of my life.

Clara: Why? Because your marriage broke? (LOL)

Stephen: Because of what happened between us. (smiley face)

Clara: What happened between us? (LOL)

Stephen: It was my first time.

Clara: I could see that.

Stephen: Seriously, I have never touched a woman ever.

Clara: I know!

Stephen: How did you understand?

Clara: You were shivering, and sucking me the whole time. (LOL)

Stephen: I love breasts!

Clara: I could see that. (LOL)

Stephen: Are you making fun of me?

Clara: No, sweetheart. I am only saying that I knew this was your first time. The way you were hungrily eating me (smiley face)

Stephen: I am no good right?

Clara: Women like me would love a guy like you, who wants to explore; but a new girl would want you to kill her (LOL). You need to learn a lot before you get married. Good this marriage broke, now you will have ample time to do your homework before you touch your wife.

Stephen: Can't we get married?

no reply from the other end...

Stephen: I asked you a question...

Clara: My baby just woke up. Catch up later.

Stephen: ok.

After about 15 minutes...

Stephen: Hi. You never answered my question

No reply from the other end...

Stephen: Avoiding me or is it because you also don't want me like all the others? Or is it because I am not rich?

No reply from the other end...

I slept that night all confused. Why wasn't Clara replying to me? Is she angry? Did I say something wrong to her?

I felt sad and guilty suddenly, some kind of tension; I slowly pulled out my wallet and took out Rachel's picture. I was not able to look at her picture because of the guilt within me.

I wanted to tell Jimmy about my first encounter, I wanted to tell him how beautiful the feeling was. I missed our dear friend Sahu. I am sure he was watching all this from a distance. I wanted to tell Jimmy everything but this was supposed to be a secret, Clara's and my secret. Our beautiful secret! *Eyes closed slowly and sound sleep.*

Chapter 12

I was all excited to tell Jimmy about my first-time experience. I would not be disclosing the name or any details, but I wanted to tell him that it did happen and so I decided to call him.

I pulled out his contact details from my phone and dialed.

Stephen: Hello!

Other side: Yes?

Stephen: Could I speak to Jimmy?

Other side: Silence...

Stephen: Is this Jimmy's house?

Other side: Yes... it is, but...

Stephen: This is an overseas call. Can you please call Jimmy; this is Stephen from Dubai.

Other side: Jimmy is no more...

Stephen: What?

Other side: Jimmy passed away last week. (*silence*)

I quickly disconnected the phone and called my Daddy.

Stephen: Hello, Daddy. I just called Jimmy. I called him on his Mumbai number and the person who picked up the call said that Jimmy is no more and that he passed away. Can you please call his uncle in Kochi and verify this information and let me know?

Daddy: Someone might have played a prank on you or maybe you were calling the wrong number. He called here last week and was enquiring about you; he even asked when were you going to come back etc. He even took down your contact details.

Stephen: Did he say anything other than that?

Daddy: No that's it. He never said anything else. Anyway, I will call his uncle's office at Marine drive. I will call you back in a while.

After a few minutes, Daddy called me, I disconnected his called and called him back as usual.

Stephen: Daddy! What happened?

Daddy: It is true. He passed away last week. He had a stroke and then he collapsed.

Stephen: hmm... (*silence*) Ok, Daddy, thanks. I will call you in the evening. I am at the office now. Convey my regards to Mummy.

Daddy: Ok. (*call disconnected*)

My friend was gone. My best friend was no more, my friend in crime was no more. The one who introduced me to the internet was gone. Both Jimmy and Sahu were in a better place now, free from all the worldly issues and at peace; both of them would be looking at me from a distance.

I lost both my friends. We were together since the 4th grade in boarding school. They both left; leaving me alone.

Chapter 13

It was that time of my life when Orkut was replaced by Facebook. Not having a personal computer or a laptop and spending money in an internet café was still a luxury. One day Clara showed me her friends from her school days. She showed me how the whole thing worked and she helped me open an account on Facebook. It was quite interesting, as many of my classmates were already registered on Facebook so it was much easier to find most of them. "I miss Jimmy and Sahu," I told Clara.

Clara and I had become very close to each other. We were more than friends but we never had a meaty experience after that night in her car, and maybe that was the reason why our friendship was so strong. We both respected each other and there were no hard and set rules between us. We shared everything with each other. It is just that we never took the sex subject to the next level.

She as usual kept on advising me that I should not be taking up someone else's financial burdens and I kept on trying to convince her that the "someone" whom she was referring to here was none other than my Daddy. She would never get convinced and the argument would continue.

I usually checked my Facebook on Clara's laptop. She even knew my password. One day I received an SMS from Clara.

Clara: Surprise... Surprise!

Stephen: What?

Clara: You have a friend request on Facebook.

Stephen: What? Who?

Clara: Some Rachel (LOL)

Stephen: What is she saying?

Clara: It is just a friend request. (LOL)

Stephen: Can we meet today evening after work?

Clara: Sure, will pass by your place.

Stephen: Ok, thanks.

Work that day in the office was hectic than usual. I had quite a few inquiries to be sent out. I had about 5 sets of quotations for which I had to prepare comparison tables and I had a few LPOs to be released as well.

Our HR Manager walked into our department and accompanying her was a lady; quite a hot woman, she looked just like a model.

HR: This is Katarina and she is from Ukraine. She will be working in this department from now on as a Secretary. Stephen, please help her with everything here. Katarina this is Stephen. He will show you everything

Stephen: Sure... Hi, Katarina.

Katarina: Hi, Stephen.

Katarina was so beautiful that guys from other departments peeped in to have a view of her. She was slim, tall, had blue eyes, and was blonde. It was her first day and I explained to her about the work we do at the Purchase Department. I handed over a copy of the Procurement Policy and the Work Flow Manual to her as well. She had a pretty face but she was not quite smart. I could tell so because she hardly understood what I was trying to teach her.

Katarina: Where are you from, Stephen?

Stephen: I am from India, Kerala.

Katarina: Ah, ok. I am from Ukraine.

Stephen: Yeah... I heard.

Katarina: Where do you stay?

Stephen: I stay near Clock Tower, near the Sahib Masjid.

Katarina: I stay close to the clock tower as well, near the Zara Hospital. How do you go home after work?

Stephen: I use the company's transportation.

Katarina: Why? Don't you drive?

Stephen: Not yet but will soon be able to. Currently, I am in the process of obtaining my driving license.

Katarina: I will pick and drop you from now on as we both have to come and leave from the same office.

Stephen: No... That's ok.

Katarina: Hey, come on. What is wrong? Just come with me, there are so many here who come with their friends to work.

Stephen: Yeah, I know but I don't want to depend on anyone. Later on, that will become an issue.

Katarina: Oh please, Stephen, just come with me for a couple of days and if you are not comfortable then you can go back to your transportation; moreover, why do you want to spend about 200 dhs on the company transportation, you can save that money right?

Stephen: Why would you want to do pick and drop services for me free of cost?

Katarina: See, I don't stay far away from your place and I will be using my car anyways, then why not just pick you up as well.

Stephen: ok, let's see.

Katarina: Oh my God! (*sighing*) It is so difficult to convince you about something. (*chuckle*)

That evening Katarina dropped me at my place and she said that she would pick me up for work on Sunday as well. She said she would call me in the weekend to confirm the time for the pickup. She was a strange woman, not sure why she wanted to do such favors for me; anyway, I always could go back to my company transportation.

That evening Clara was supposed to come and meet me. She was supposed to show me Rachel's friend request on her laptop. However, Clara was busy in the office and she could not make it and so I went to one of the internet cafés and looked up my Facebook account. There was already a message for me from Rachel which said–

"At last I found you..."

I was kind of surprised by her message. I never ever thought that she would message me; I hurriedly accepted her friend request and opened up her profile page and started reading her posts and I also looked into her photos. My dear Rachel, she was not the old Rachel I knew. She was all grown up. She looked even more beautiful now. The girl had completely changed; in her photos, she wore revealing clothes and showed off her sexy cleavages, smoking, drinking, and whatnot. I was not very happy seeing those pictures, but I was happy that she came this time looking for me. She had pierced her ears now; she never wore earrings in school except on our farewell day, the one which I had bought her.

That night Clara called me...

Clara: So you accepted her friend request huh? (*chuckles*)

Stephen: Yeah!

Clara: She is hot man; my God!

Stephen: She was not like this before.

Clara: What do you mean? She stays in Canada and how do you expect her to dress up? Come on, Stephen, people change; but she is hot—sizzling hot; her tits are quite big from what I can see (*laughing*), you will for sure love them. (*chuckles*)

Stephen: Do you think that would ever happen? The day she comes to know that I am still struggling she will immediately unfriend me.

Clara: Everyone is not like Ann, ok. What if God wants you to have her, and what if your prayers are being answered?

Stephen: Yeah...let's see

Clara: Hey, but go slow yeah. Don't just hurry and ruin everything.

I told Clara about Katarina and her pick and drop offer. Clara educated me that hot girls always would want a harmless guy like me to accompany them, like a bodyguard so that no guys would unnecessarily come forward to talk to her. I got Clara's point and maybe she was right.

Later that evening I sat and thought to myself as to why did Rachel say "at last I found you". What did she mean by that? I liked the earrings she was wearing and I remembered the days just before our farewell day at school.

I heard my classmates making fun of Rachel in the boys' dormitory. She had asked one of them to buy her a clip earring so that she could wear it along with her farewell sari. It was not possible for any student to go out of school other than with our parents; the other occasion we were taken out was to the airport to go to our homes for our vacations. The teachers could go out once a week. I wanted to somehow buy this clip earring for Rachel and so I decided to approach our dance teacher who liked me a lot. I told her that Rachel had not pierced her ears and she wanted a clip earring to wear on our farewell day. Our farewell day was on a Sunday and the dance teacher could go out of the school only on Sunday as well. The dance teacher knew that I loved Rachel like crazy and agreed to buy a pair of clip earrings and hand it over to her.

That evening, Rachel wore the earrings given to her by our dance teacher. She looked very pretty. I hope she liked it! I could never ask her ever until this moment if she liked those earrings. The last thing I knew was that those earrings were handed over to Rachel a few hours before the function and she was very happy until she heard that it was from me. She refused to take them when she heard that they were from my end; however, she wore it later when our dance teacher forced her.

Chapter 14

Six years in the gulf and things, surroundings, and situations had changed in my life. So it was holiday time once again, but this time there was a slight change—I would never have any banks or people chasing me for any money that my Daddy owed them anymore. My Daddy was debt-free; instead of him it was me now, the only difference was that my lenders were banks in the UAE and they would not bother me as long as my salary was credited into my Salary Account with them from where a chunk of money from my salary was being deducted as loan installment. I was happy because my Daddy and Mummy were happy; at least they could live in peace.

I called up Clara and told her that I was going down to India for a month and she offered to drop me at the Airport on the departure day and also to pick me up from the airport when I arrived back; she was a darling. I loved her more than anything, but she was different. She always thought that I had a long way to go and that she should never ever allow me to get stuck to her and spoil my bright future. I was ready to marry her but she would never ever let me bring that topic up. She was a very nice person and I loved her a lot.

Clara and I met the day before my departure day. We talked for a long time at her place; her folks had all gone for vacation as well and she was alone with her daughter in the house. This meeting was unlike our usual meetings as we decided to stay home and she decided to cook for me. She had decided to make mutton biriyani for dinner. We had a few beers ready for the evening which was chilling in her fridge and we decided to see a movie together that night as well, but the highlight was that she wanted me to stay at her place that night and I accepted the offer.

So we both were in the kitchen making biriyani. I was a good cook myself and the biriyani came out well; we had our beers and we watched a movie as planned. It was quite late by then and Zoyie was already asleep. Clara carried her to their bed and tucked her in the cozy quilt.

Then we both walked to their balcony. The warm breeze hit our faces, the lights on the balcony were switched off and it was dark everywhere and there was pin-drop silence around.

She moved closer to me, her shoulders touched mine, and then we spoke a lot about our lives. We spoke about how she used to teach me the names of cars from her balcony when I was a child, and how I was not a child anymore. She was sure that my parents would get me married soon and I would have a life of my own then. I again asked her if I could marry her but then she refused to speak about it, almost changed the topic immediately.

Clara: Hey you want to watch the TV? I am going for a shower.

Stephen: Sure!

We both got back into the apartment and Clara closed the balcony door and went to her room. I saw her taking her towel and get into the washroom, but she had not closed the door.

I was not sure if that was an indication that she wanted me to accompany her; with a lot of courage I walked up to her bedroom, Zoyie was asleep and I could hear the water jet out of the shower inside the shower room. The door was slightly opened but not locked from inside; I could see her behind the shower curtain, I slowly opened the door a little more and the door squeaked. She immediately moved the shower curtain slightly and looked at me. There was silence and she switched off the tap and started applying soap on her naked body ignoring my presence in the washroom. I slowly walked up to the shower curtain and moved it slightly, she was naked and she looked so beautiful. Her buttocks were round and curvy and her shoulders and back were so pretty. I could see her full body without having to pull down her bra and unbuttoning her blouse. She still ignored my presence, and then slowly asked me in a soft voice. "Want to have a shower?"

I quickly removed my clothes and got into the shower with her. I was standing right behind her–my body touching hers, she could feel my male hardness touching her buttocks trying to find its way between them. She caught my male hardness with her bare hands tightly; which made it even more erect and hard. I kissed her wet shoulders and bit behind her ears slowly, my hands clasped her breasts and her stomach. I felt her rubbery nipples between my fingers and she moaned as I pressed them between my fingers. She was stroking my penis with her hands in a rhythmic motion holding it tight. I then slowly ran my fingers further down to her navel until I could feel her pubic hair between her thighs, I drove my finger into her wet softness and she immediately turned around towards me and hugged me tightly. She was breathing heavily, she whispered in my ears kissing me at the same time "do me please" still panting. She was kind of pleading me. I got out of the shower pulling her hands, pulling her down onto the carpet of her bedroom. I kissed her beautiful lips hungrily while groping her wet breasts with my hands. She whispered in my ears "slowly, it hurts...and don't go fast" and then I went down and sucked at her black rubbery nipples, rotating my tongue around her large areola. I sucked at both her breast, slowly biting them now and then, my bites made her moan and shudder. Her wetness had now increased and she literally pulled my face to hers kissing my lips and told me " just get into me...kill me please" and she lifted her legs while I got in between them, she held my male hardness in her hands and guided it towards her softness, and I was entering her and I was in her. My first intercourse ever was with my first love, the woman of my dreams from my childhood days. She was so warm and soft and juicy from within. I was moving in and out of her and she was moaning louder now. She was squeezing my buttocks pressing them towards her body and we both were sweating and were wet and breathing hard. Suddenly, there was a burst inside her and she held me tight clasping her legs around my waist, I was locked between her legs, not being able to move any further, I still forced myself to move in and out of her.

Her whole body rising up and down as she was having an orgasm. I stopped and kissed her; she smiled and said, "I feel like a woman again now." She was breathing heavily. She then slowly let loose her body and lifted up her legs for me. I penetrated her softness again; she was so full, warm and wet, she placed both my hands on her breast and smiled, and then I moved in and out of her. I squeezed her breasts to get a hold on her to balance my body and she was moaning and then I exploded inside her. I was breathing hard, and she wiped the sweat and water which was dripping from my forehead. My penis was still in her while I slept on her breast.

That night we played with each other's bodies, exploring each other shamelessly. She taught me a lot about a woman's body. She taught me about foreplay and educated me on how I had to lick and eat a vagina and suck at the clitoris gently to arouse her or any other woman for that matter. She also educated me on foreplay tricks a woman had to administer or had to do with her mouth to her man. I made love to her several times that night; trying all the new ways that I had learned from her and the little things I knew from the books I had read and the movies I had seen. She put up that whole night with my silliness; she loved the way I wanted to try different styles, and she laughed when I failed miserably, yet understanding my urge, yet not taking any part of my inquisitiveness in an offensive way. I kept touching her and sucking and kissing her breasts until we both slept.

In the morning, we both went out and bought a few things for me to take back to India. She helped me pack. I had brought all my luggage from my room to her apartment. While packing I asked her, "Can I marry you?"

Clara: Again the same topic?

Stephen: Why? We are just like husband and wife now right?

Clara: No sweetheart, some things are just not meant to be; our love for each other is special, and let that be a secret. You need to get married to a very nice girl, don't hurt your parents by marrying a woman like me. Sure they have dreams about your wedding and life. I will always be there for you; I am not going anywhere

Stephen: I love you, Clara, please; let's just get married, to hell with what others would think.

Clara: I am living this life for my daughter and that's it.

She hugged me and kissed me on my forehead and said, "You are very special to me and I want to see you grow big and successful."

That evening I felt very heavy while leaving her at the departure lounge; tears rolled down my cheeks as I walked towards the departure area. Never did I feel like that before especially when going home for a vacation. I looked back wanting to see her one more time before I passed the baggage check-in area, she was crying as well, wiping her tears.

I was happy that I was going home but was sad that I would not be able to see my dear mate, my everything.

Chapter 15

The pilot said, "cabin crew, please take your seats for landing". I could see greenery everywhere, as the aircraft was descending I could see the streams and water bodies and then soon it was so green everywhere; I had reached my territory, my motherland. Then there was a thud sound and the aircraft shook and shuddered; the tires of the aircraft had touched the runway and after a few minutes the aircraft reduced its speed and soon was connected to the jetway. The pilot again announced a few things like the local time and the current temperature outside etc. to which I was paying no attention to, the only thing I heard correctly was "thank you for flying with us".

While waiting for my luggage to arrive at the conveyer belt, I quickly switched on my mobile phone, there were 3 messages, I quickly opened them. Two of them were from Clara and the last one was from Idea, one of the local mobile network companies. I quickly opened Clara's messages.

1st SMS from Clara: Did you reach? Hope you had a nice flight.

2nd SMS from Clara: Please reply... I will be waiting for your message.

I was so happy to see her message and replied—

"Yes, just landed, waiting for my luggage; will message you when I reach home. Miss you already."

In a few seconds, I received another SMS from Clara.

"Miss you too; be safe and enjoy yourself."

I smiled, in the meantime, I could see my luggage coming towards me on the conveyer belt. I quickly collected all my baggage and exited the Kochi International Airport. My Daddy was waiting to greet me in the arrival area. I spotted him from in between the crowd and walked towards him and hugged him. It was more than a year now that we had met. We quickly got into the tourist taxi my Daddy had come to pick me up in and headed home. Home was about an hour's drive from the Airport. On the way, we talked about all the Gulf stories and experiences.

The dust and the dirt of my country felt nice; I liked the noise and the broken roads. I told Daddy to stop at a Thattukada (roadside shop), I wanted to have a cup of tea. The driver stopped at a small Thattukada on the way. I liked the untidiness of the shop. I was given a small glass filled with piping hot Chaya (tea). The tea tasted great. My Daddy and the car driver were shocked to see me enjoying the tea. I was in my country and I loved everything about it. This time my vacation felt different; my family and I were free of all the debt in my country. I was a free bird in my motherland.

Mummy was very happy to see me. She had prepared my favorite dishes– Pidi and Chicken Curry. Pidi is a Kerala delicacy made out of rice powder and grated coconut, and I loved it. I was ordered by Mummy to have a quick shower. The water in my home felt different; I felt renewed with every drop of it on my body.

After having the delicious food cooked by my Mummy, we all sat together to talk and to open the things that I had brought from Dubai. In Kerala, we call it "Gelf products" which included chocolates especially Quality Street-Macintosh, perfumes, bathing soaps, hair shampoos, face creams, Tiger Balm, Axe Oil, Niddo milk powder, orange-flavored Tang, etc.

I had bought a gold bangle for Mummy this time; the poor thing did not have any gold ornaments to wear.

I bought Daddy a wristwatch, quite an expensive one. They both were extremely happy. I wanted to tell them that all of these were Clara's selections but I didn't.

I sent Clara an SMS later...

Stephen: I reached home safely; just finished dinner, very tired.

Clara: Ok, sleep then if you are tired; good night.

Stephen: Good night, I will call you tomorrow.

Clara: It's ok, call only if you can, just SMS me otherwise

Stephen: yeah ok... bye!

After a long time, I was lying down on my bed, happy and content. Everything felt different this time. I was sleeping in my own house; I needn't have to worry anymore about the bank loan taken pledging my home. I was at peace; except that I was thinking about Clara. Why was she not allowing me to marry her? That night I decided that I was going to tell Daddy and Mummy about her before the vacation was over; probably Clara would accept my proposal if they spoke to her; but how was I going to start the topic? I was confused; what if Clara said no to my proposal? Will I be able to bear another rejection?.

Chapter 16

My parents were all set to find a bride for me this time. They had a few marriage brokers who were experts in arranged marriages as per our tradition, ready to take me and my parents to see potential brides. So I was made to dress up nicely, the perfumes which I had brought as part of the "Gelf products" was showered on me. A tourist taxi was hired, and the broker was ready to take us for bride visits. It was so embarrassing, all of this was unnecessary if Clara would have nodded yes to my proposal. With guilt in my mind, I decided to go with them. I knew what I had in my mind and meeting potential brides knowing that my answer would be always a "No" was sheer waste of time. I quickly sent an SMS to Clara–

Stephen: They are taking me to visit some potential brides today.

Clara: Good, select someone nice and pretty.

Stephen: Are you sure you don't want to tell me anything else?

Clara: Yes love, just go and see if you like someone.

Stephen: You know what I want right, then why are you letting me do this?

Clara: We have discussed this many times dear, now don't keep them waiting just go.

Stephen: Then why did you cry at the airport if you have no feelings for me?

Clara: I never cried...

Stephen: Really?

Clara: I will call you in the evening I am heading for a meeting; be a good boy and go with your Daddy and Mummy now. Bye!

Stephen: Please...

I never got a reply after that from Clara.

The first potential bride

We walked into a small house, there were Father and Mother of the potential bride who greeted us in the house, very soon the girl was introduced to me. I was there only for the sake of my parents and was not actually interested in seeing any potential bride. To be honest, the girl was kind of cute, but she looked very small for me; but that could be the Clara effect as I would like to call it.

Tea and biscuits along with some *ladoos* were served and then there was a question and answer session. The 1ˢᵗ question was from the father of the potential bride–

Bride's Father: Where do you work?

Stephen: I work for the Sharjah Government

Bride's Father: What is your salary?

Stephen: (*looking puzzled and shocked*) About 5000 dirhams.

Bride's Father: How much is that in India?

Stephen: About 60,000 Rupees.

Bride's Father: Will you take my daughter to Dubai after marriage?

Stephen: I can sponsor my wife. (*I said it in a very diplomatic way*)

Bride's Father: Which car do you own?

Stephen: I have not got my driving license yet, but I am learning... Almost there...

Bride's Father: I meant here, which car do you own in Kerala? Clearly that Tourist vehicle is not your own car.

Stephen: I don't have a car here either; We had a few vehicles but had to sell them due to some financial issues.

I just wanted to run out of that house, wanted to go back to my cave in Sharjah, wanted to be safe in Clara's arms. I did not like to be a part of this circus. I was very disappointed after coming out of that house. Daddy explained to me that this was normal and that the girl's family would question me about a lot of things, and I would have to answer them. I refused to meet any more girls but Daddy and Mummy insisted and so did the broker.

I was then taken to the second house.

The second potential bride

This is a slightly bigger house than the last one and there were so many people in that house and I was nervous seeing all of them. We were greeted as usual into the house and I was kind of getting uncomfortable because of all the people in that house. I felt that they were taking all this too seriously. The potential bride's father was introducing me to the entire family which made me feel even more uncomfortable. Then they called the potential bride and a girl walked in wearing a traditional Kerala saree. She was quite pretty. Her body shape was quite defined in that saree of hers. She was kind of really nice, and then she was told to bring in her mark sheet and her qualification certificates by her father. She sweetly showed me all her certificates to which I was constantly saying "all this is not required", however, the girl's father insisted that I see all of them. After some time, we were invited to their dining room and there was so much food and snacks kept on the table and I was like I just want a cup of coffee and that's it, but then I was forced to have something to eat and then I opted for the beef cutlet that was kept in one corner. I quickly ate it and went back to the drawing room while my parents and the broker were interacting with the family members. I sat quietly in the drawing room for them to finish so that we could just leave the premises, suddenly, one of the uncles of the potential bride asked me if I would like to speak to Tina (potential bride) and as a reply to that, I said it was not necessary, however, the uncle insisted that I speak to Tina in private as she wanted to speak to me. I was taken to Tina's room away from the dining table. Tina was already waiting for me there in her room. I was having mixed feelings about all this as I was not used to such situations.

Tina: Hi! (quickly getting up from her bed on seeing me enter the room)

Stephen: Hi!

Tina: How are you, Stephen?

Stephen: I am good, Tina. That's your name, isn't it?

Tina: Yes, so you liked me?

I didn't know how to reply to that question because this was the first time ever someone has asked me such a question. Usually, I keep telling all the women that I loved them and nothing has ever worked out, however, this was the first time that it was happening the other way round. I replied in a low tone.

Stephen: You are quite pretty Tina and well-educated.

Tina: and hot? (*grinning*)

Stephen: Yeah...not bad. (*chuckles*)

Tina: So are you going to marry me; tell me the truth?

Stephen: I am not sure. (*confused face*)

Tina: Any girlfriends?

I was shocked hearing that question and it literally showed on my face. I didn't know what to say. I was like should I say about Clara or should I talk about Rachel, Not knowing what to say.

Stephen: err...

Tina: What's her name? (*grinning*)

Stephen: Chuckles...no there is no one like that.

Tina: So there was... you mean to say? (*still smiling*)

Stephen: How about you? Boyfriends?

Tina: I was wondering if you would ask. (*smiling*) Yes, I have had so many affairs but nothing serious except for one college love. It was the talk of the college; hmm I know what you want to ask, you might want to know if we were sexually active, isn't it?

Stephen: no please, you don't need to tell me all this.

Tina: Really? You sure you don't want to know?

Stephen: Yeah 100%.

Tina: Have you had sex ever or are you a virgin. I mean fresher? (*grinning*)

Stephen: Not really. I mean... (*surprised at the question*)

Tina: Don't have to tell me...I can see it on your face (*teasing smile*)

Stephen: What? I mean what do you mean?

Tina: You from Dubai right so it might have been a prostitute or are you a professional in this huh? I mean many women? Twosome? Threesome? (*laughing*)

I was enjoying her conversation and was liking her actually, her frankness and smartness.

Tina: So which ones are the best Russian, Lebanese, or the ones from the Philippines? Do you want a tissue? Why are you sweating so much (*teasing smile*) Ok relax... Have a tissue. (*handing me a box of tissue*)

Stephen: How did you come up with the assumption that I have slept with so many women?

Tina: I didn't say that... I was only asking you (*grinning*) and by the way, didn't you notice something on my certificates?

Stephen: What?

Tina: Ok... So you were not looking. (*chuckles*) I have majored in psychology.

Stephen: No wonder you are asking so many questions.

Tina: So, my assessment is that you are the average kind of guy, good and well-behaved; never got angry with any of my questions, quite pure from within, and since you are never going to ask me the question if I liked you or found you attractive or not, let me tell you the answer myself. You are quite hot, good-looking, quite handsome and I really like you. But to be honest, I am slightly too much for a person like you. We both will have an immediate connection because as the saying goes opposites get attracted faster, but in the long run you will get fed-up with me. You will start hating me by the time we spend a few years together.

Stephen: It was nice meeting you, and I don't think I will ever be able to forget you.

Tina: Same here. All the best though; and one more thing, you deserve someone better than me. (*smiling*)

I was quite impressed with this woman's behavior; but as she said, she is too smart for me, I might get tied up, but I loved this particular experience. I never felt like that before and this was the first time a woman had said that she liked me and felt that I was attractive.

Then we headed to the last house. I was very tired, but the broker insisted that we go to see this one more girl.

The third potential bride

We went through a shabby gate. It was a very small house; not well-maintained and there was this normal family—a Father, Mother a daughter, and a younger son. I was greeted with respect. The house was not at all fancy or painted, the walls looked quite shabby, and the family was also not very nicely dressed. I had a feeling that we were at the wrong house at one point. However, the regular scenario began, tea was served along with some snacks. I was tired of drinking tea and eating since morning but I drank the tea and ate the snacks. I didn't want them to feel offended in any way. The girl looked very thin, malnourished; and the normally expected questioning did not seem to come this time. The potential Bride's father was talking to my parents more than me...

Bride's Father: Sir, (addressing my Daddy), we are not in a good position financially to send our girl to your family. My girl will take care of your house like her own and will take care of you and Madam like how she takes care of us.

It looked as though he was pleading with us to take her daughter in marriage. I felt bad for the girl who was listening to this conversation lifelessly. However, luckily I was not asked to speak to this potential bride and we exited from their house as soon as possible.

I was happy that the day's tour was over and that I was heading home, the broker asked us—

Broker: So, did you find anyone suitable?

Stephen: We will let you know, thank you.

Broker: the First and the Second seems to be good; however, I will have to ask them their opinion as well.

Stephen: Yeah, you can let us know their opinion.

Broker: But which one do you think was good enough?

Stephen: ahh... (sighing) We will call you; I indicated Daddy to pay him his fees and to get rid of him from the vehicle.

Daddy quietly asked the driver to stop at the corner of the road and gave the Broker some cash and told him that we would let him know by tomorrow.

Later in the evening, there was a discussion about the girls between me and my parents. We all had a common selection the Second Potential Bride "Tina"; but then I knew for sure that it would be a "No" from Tina's side.

I SMS'd Clara about the day's meeting minutes, and she said she would call me in a while. I kept waiting for her call and then after some time decided to go for a shower before having dinner and getting to bed.

My mobile phone rang, and I was in the shower, my Daddy saw that the call was from Clara, thinking that it was me Clara said—

Clara: Hi sweetheart, how was your day?

Daddy: Hello, Clara, how are you?

Clara: *silence...* Hello, Daddy; how are you? How is Mummy?

Daddy: All are fine here; how is your family?

Clara: Everyone is fine; Stephen keeps telling me about you all always.

Daddy: How is your husband? You have one daughter, right?

Clara: Everyone is fine (*sounding nervous*); yes, one daughter, Zoyie.

Daddy: How old is she?

Clara: She is 10 years old now.

Daddy: Stephen keeps telling about you and Zoyie.

Clara: Ah... (*confused*) Where is Stephen?

Daddy: He is having a shower; will ask him to call you back.

Clara: Ok Daddy, bye Daddy, please convey my regards to Mummy.

Daddy: Sure, ok bye. (*phone disconnected*)

I sent an SMS to Clara.

Stephen: Where are you? Heard you had a conversation with Daddy?

Clara: Yesss, send me an SMS when you are not around your parents.

Stephen: Yeah ok...but what happened, did Daddy say anything?

Clara: No nothing, just call me when you are alone.

Stephen: Yeah ok.

Later that night I kissed my parents goodnight and went to my room and sent an SMS to Clara.

Stephen: Hey... I am alone now.

After a few seconds...

Clara: Hi...ok. I will call you now.

(mobile phone ringing)

Stephen: Hi...tell me...what happened?

Clara: Nothing Sweets...Daddy was asking me about everyone here, about my husband, Zoyie etc.

Stephen: And...what did you say?

Clara: I said everyone was fine. Hey, so you have not said that I am divorced to Daddy and Mummy?

Stephen: No, I haven't.

Clara: hmm...ok tell me...did you like anyone?

Stephen: We met three girls today; the first one's father kind of insulted me.

Clara: What do you mean insulted you? (*annoyed tone*)

Stephen: He asked me how much I earn, which car I drive in UAE and which car do I own here in Kerala and what not; he asked will I be able to sponsor his daughter.

Clara: What the fuck! You could have said, "Learn to speak first and then try to fix an alliance for your daughter" and should have walked right out of that house. Stephen you should learn to speak up for yourself or everyone will take you for granted.

Stephen: All this would not have happened if someone would have said "yes!"

Clara: hmmm (*sighing*) Ok so did you like anyone from the three?

Stephen: There was this one girl, Tina; very good looking, hot, nice body...

Clara: Nice body means? better than mine?

Stephen: oh... look who is getting possessive now. (*grinning, teasing*)

Clara: Hello...I just wanted to know if she was good enough for you; I mean I know what you like and that's why I was checking.

Stephen: I believe you and 'you' is what I need.

Clara: Did she have big tits?

Stephen: hmm... She never showed me. (*laugh*)

Clara: Very funny, tell me fast, this is an international call and you are wasting my money.

Stephen: Yeah, she had quite big ones I think. She is fair, nice lips, nice hips...

Clara: How do you know that?

Stephen: She was wearing a saree, and in a saree, you get to see the curves; and she had a nice ass as well.

Clara: hmm (*sighing*)

Stephen: But she cannot be compared to you. She is nowhere even close to your sexiness, you are so dynamic and classy. A bomb actually. (*teasing*)

Clara: Really? You think so?

Stephen: Yes! And moreover, she was extra smart; she could kind of read my mind? She has majored in psychology, so she was literally grilling me; and at the end of the session, she told me that I was good-looking and handsome and that she liked me very much...

Clara: oh... (*silence*)

Stephen: However, she also said that I was not a match for her and that I deserved someone better, and we parted ways. Luckily, Daddy and Mummy also liked her from the three; but I am sure it is going to be a negative response from Tina's family and so I am safe. (*laughing*)

Clara: hmm, ok what next? Are there any more bride visits lined up?

Stephen: Clara please, just one word from your end and we can end this. We can stop this circus; I love you, and I cannot think of an other women in my life, please try to understand.

Clara: Stephen, do you know why my marriage broke?

Stephen: I don't care, I am only worried about our life and our future and I am least interested in your past.

Clara: You have to know something. The main reason for my divorce was that my husband felt that I was a slut, wearing revealing clothes for work, coming back late from work after meetings. He assumed that I was fucking someone the whole time. You won't understand Stephen how it feels, my husband would forcefully sticks his finger into my vagina to smell it, to see if he gets any smell of semen or the fresh smell of soap just incase I have washed up. He literally beat me up and used to rape me after that. (*sound of crying*)

Stephen: Why are you crying? That is all over, right?

Clara: It is not over. Do you know what would happen if I marry you? Well, the day I do that all that he had said in court would come true. Marrying a boy who is almost 10 years younger than me would become a sensation, and he will use that in court to get custody of my daughter. He is waiting for a chance. (*crying*)

Stephen: Please Clara stop crying; we will figure out some way or the other.

Clara: There is no way out until my daughter turns 18 years of age, and then she would be able to decide whom to stay with. I don't want my daughter even going next to her father.

Stephen: We will wait until then, just tell me once my dear.

Clara: Fuck Stephen, you don't understand, I don't want you to spoil your fuckin life waiting for me you dammit! (*crying*)

Stephen: But why?

Clara: Because.... because... I love you... you IDIOT! (*crying*) I love you a lot...

Stephen: Stop crying, please...

Clara: Ok bye... I will call you tomorrow, I need to go...

Stephen: Clara...please...wait....don't disconnect!

Clara: bye! (*crying*) *phone disconnected*

I immediately sent an SMS.

Stephen: Clara stop crying please...I can't take this... please...

Clara: I am fine...I will call you tomorrow...but please don't force me for marriage or anything or I will stop speaking to you forever

Stephen: Ok, fine, I will not force you any more... whatever you say...now stop crying...

Clara: I am fine...don't worry, get to bed, sleep. I am sure your parents will have an agenda for tomorrow (LOL), bye, good night.

Stephen: Bye, good night, call me tomorrow...please...

Clara: I will...same time...

Stephen: Love you!

(no reply from the other end...)

Chapter 17

While having breakfast Daddy gets a call, it was the Broker, it was quite a brief call; Daddy silently came back and sat at his seat.

Mummy: Who was it?

Daddy: The Marriage Broker.

Mummy: Did he manage to speak to Tina's parents?

Daddy: Yes, they told him that Tina does not want to get married at this point and that she required more time; they have apologized to us.

Mummy: What were you both speaking (*looking at me*), it was quite a long conversation, smiling and laughing and I thought you both had a connection.

Stephen: We were just speaking normal things; it is her choice if she wants to get married or not, right?

Mummy: Then why did that broker take us there then? Wasting our time... and what were her parents thinking? (*fuming*) We are not jobless here...

Stephen: Mummy it is ok...please...

Mummy: It is not ok. (*fuming*)

Daddy: Let's stop talking about this; the girl does not want to get married now, she didn't say that she did not like him. Let's give her some more time; I will speak to her parents personally and let them know that we are interested

Stephen: Don't do that Daddy; let us respect her (*Tina's*) decision; let them call us if required.

Daddy: Ok, as you say; by the way, do you like someone?

there was a sudden silence in the room...

Stephen: Nothing like that...

Daddy: So you mean there is someone in your life already?

Stephen: I didn't say that.

Daddy: Do you still love Rachel?

Stephen: Don't think all that would work out; she is in Canada, very changed

Daddy: I did a background check about her family. Her family is all good, Rachel is their only daughter, they are settled in Qatar, they have their own business there. Rachel was sent to Canada for her higher studies and then she never came back it seems. She decided to settle there. The things which I heard about Rachel are not very pleasant, but if you still like her then we don't mind either because we don't need to know about her past we need to only care about the future... your future with her. So think properly and tell us and we can proceed.

Mummy: Life is not puppy love. (*looking at me*) You need to think properly before you decide on Rachel. Marriage does not involve just the bride and the groom alone, but it involves both the families as well. Everyone in our family knows about Rachel and the mad kind of love you had or rather have for her; so the entire family is waiting to know who you would be getting married to

Stephen: I don't care about what others or my family members think. I never saw any of these family members when we needed them the most and I am not desperate to get married now either... I will let you know when it is time

Daddy: Can I ask you a question? What is your relationship with Clara?

Stephen: We are good friends, she is always there for me whenever I need her, in fact, she is my best friend.

Daddy: Good! Friendship is good but be sure that it is nothing beyond that.

Stephen: We are good friends, Daddy. (*my face was all red and I was sweating*)

Daddy: We will not be able to look at anyone's face if you have other plans with Clara. She is very much elder than you and she has a daughter as well. I don't want her family life to be destroyed because of my son.

Stephen: She is a divorcee; it happened a few years back.

Daddy: Please, Son, don't fall into any trap, we only have you; if you take any such wrong decision then you will not see us both ever again.

Stephen: Can we please stop this topic (*speaking out loudly*); I told you, we are only friends.

Daddy: Ok, we are only telling you as we must correct or warn our Son if he is about to do something wrong.

I sent an SMS to Clara that night...

Stephen: Are you there?

Clara: Hi, will call you in 2 minutes.

Stephen: Ok!

I made sure that the door to my room was closed properly this time as I was worried that my parents could hear our conversation and that was how they came to know that I loved her. *(mobile phone ringing)*

Stephen: Hi

Clara: Hey Sweetheart, how are you?

Stephen: I am good, how about you?

Clara: You don't sound good though. What happened, is everything alright?

Stephen: Yeah...I am fine.

Clara: Decided on someone from yesterday's visits.

Stephen: None of them are going to work out.

Clara: So you are sad because of that huh... *(teasing)*

Stephen: You know me...do you think I would be sad?

Clara: You don't sound normal though, anyway, leave all that, why don't you send Rachel an e-mail?

Stephen: About what? And then she will start abusing me again.

Clara: I think she has feelings for you, the way she said "at last I found you" and all that (chuckles), just send her an e-mail asking her for her number and then you can speak to her as well. Just forget about all your past conversations and am sure she is not the old girl anymore and you are also not the same old Stephen; give here a chance, people change.

Stephen: Ok!

Clara: You have a lot of friend requests piling up on your Facebook; there is Michelle's friend request as well; shall I accept all of them for you?

Stephen: Sure, can you ask Michelle for her phone number?

Clara: Sure ok; yeah you need to get in touch with all your old friends, you never know, what if one of them is your future wife?

Stephen: Sure, ok! (*irritated*)

Clara: What happened to you? Is everything alright?

Stephen: Yeah...yeah I am fine, just tired... sleepy.

Clara: oh...ok, then good night, sleep. And don't forget to send that e-mail...make it crisp...to the point.

Stephen: Yeah ok...good night...

And I disconnected the phone

This was the first time I was speaking to Clara without any excitement. I was getting irritated by her jokes; don't know what I should be doing. I was so happy and at peace. This holiday is really killing me now. I am disturbed, worried.

e-mail to Rachel

Dear Rachel,

Hope you are fine, my parents want me to get married, and so I thought I need to ask you before I make a decision. I still love you from all my heart like the way in our school days. I am attaching my current photograph along with this e-mail.

I work for the Sharjah Government now; nothing big but doing well by God's Grace. If you are looking for someone rich then I am not the guy. I am not at all rich.

If you are interested, then please send me the details of your parents so that I could get my parents to speak to them.

Let me know your thoughts.

Regards,

Stephen.

Reply from Rachel

Hi Stephen,

I am flattered to know that you still love me. You are a very nice person, but I have a lot of commitments, moreover, I have not even thought about marriage at this point in my life.

Marriage is nowhere on the agenda currently and I don't think our wavelengths match. I am not the Rachel you knew back in school anymore, things have changed in my life.

Anyway, thank you so much for the e-mail.

Bye.

Reply to Rachel

Hi,

I can understand that you have commitments, why don't we sort out all of them together? I am not sure if I can sort out all your issues but I can promise that I will hold your hand through all those commitments and we could sort things out.

I am ready to wait for you until you think it is time. You just have to let me know and I don't want to know anything about your past. I am only interested in our future together.

Let me know.

Regards,

Stephen.

Reply from Rachel

Dude,

I know you love me a lot and I am thankful for that but please understand that I am not the typical Malayali girl anymore. If you are north pole then I am south pole, that is the kind of wavelength we have.

Sorry but my answer is "No".

Bye.

Rejections were a usual thing in my life; everyone liked me but no one wanted to marry me. This vacation was bad, I just wanted to go back.

SMS *received on my phone...*

Clara: Michelle's mobile number...0091-968752231

Stephen: Thanks!

Clara: Did you send an e-mail to Rachel?

Stephen: No...didn't feel like.

I started telling lies to Clara for the first time; I did not want to share my failure stories with her anymore.

Clara: Why?

Stephen: I will send her one later, need to go to the internet café for that.

Clara: ah...ok, call Michelle then but don't commit anything to anyone unless you hear back from Rachel. I have a strong feeling that Rachel is going to say 'yes'.

I just wanted to yell out the truth that I am useless and no one wanted me; I wanted to tell Clara that it was a big "no" from Rachel.

Stephen: Thanks, you take care of yourself!

Clara: You too...bye.

Stephen: Bye!

Dialed Michelle's number....

Michelle: Hello!

Stephen: Hi...remember my voice?

Michelle: Stephen! Oh my gosh! Never thought that you would call me so fast.

Stephen: So? How are you?

Michelle: All good going on; how is Dubai?

Stephen: Dubai is good; are you in Kochi now?

Michelle: No, I am in Bangalore, I work here for a consultancy firm in the HR Department.

Stephen: I called to tell you something...

Michelle: Yeah go on...

Stephen: My parents want me to get married so before I said yes to anyone I thought I need to ask all my friends first. I would like to get married to you Michelle. If you are interested I could ask my parents to speak to your parents.

Michelle: Wow... I never thought that you would ever ask me such a question in my life. I need to ask my parents, Stephen. Can I call you back by tomorrow evening? (*sighing*)

Stephen: Sure, Michelle, take your time, by the way, can I have Ziya's phone number?

Michelle: She is not the old Ziya anymore; she is a National Award winner today.

Stephen: You both are in touch right?

Michelle: Yes, but I will have to ask her permission to give her number to you.

Stephen: Oh...ok, just tell her that I enquired about her, and also tell her that I am very happy for her.

Michelle: Sure!

Stephen: Ok... bye then.

Michelle: Bye! (*phone disconnected*)

Later that day I went to my family church. I spent a lot of time praying, crying. I told my Lord whatever I had to. I complained like a child about my life, that no one wanted me, I was kind of becoming desperate, begging everyone I knew to marry me. Such a pathetic situation! None of my prayers were ever answered, but I knew my Lord had my back and I knew that someday all my pains would be taken away, all my hard work would pay and all my prayers would be answered. With a heavy heart, I went into the cemetery where my ancestors and my grandparents were laid to rest. We had a family tomb, and I paid a visit to my ancestors always, whenever I got a chance. As usual, I burnt candles in front of the tombstone and prayed. I always felt the warmth and love whenever I visited my ancestors. This time was no different, except that I could not control my emotions and I burst out unable to control my tears. I begged the souls around me to pray for me to the Lord Almighty. If they were listening; I begged them to bless this child of theirs.

When I came out of the church I saw Ann with her husband at a distance, she was pregnant. I did not want to show myself to her, I was actually embarrassed, I was nothing in front of her. She was getting into her expensive car, obviously, she married someone rich unlike me a big zero. She looked happy, what else did I need. I told to myself, as long as everyone is happy, I am happy as well. That day I realized that I had nothing, and I was alone. Was I actually happy? And my heart yelled within me "no!" But something from within told me that everything was going to be fine.

My phone rang...it was Michelle...

Stephen: Hello...

Michelle: Hi, Stephen, how are you?

Stephen: I am good, how about you?

Michelle: Good, well... I spoke to my parents and the answer is "no". Sorry, Stephen, I cannot go against my parents; I always loved you a lot and I always will.

Stephen: I expected the same. (*teasing myself*)

Michelle: Really?

Stephen: Yeah, hey did you speak to Ziya?

Michelle: Yes I did, but she said not to give her number to anyone, she is very busy with her career and she does not want any distractions. Stephen, frankly speaking, we both love you equally from within but we value our friendship with each other more. If one of us decides to settle down with you then our friendship from so many years would end and be destroyed. So we decided that we both will not have any relationship with you as we value our friendship with each other more than anything else. We can be good friends like in the school days, Stephen.

Stephen: I respect your decision, convey my regards to your parents and to Ziya and her parents as well.

Michelle: Keep in touch, Stephen; just one more thing to add, you have an awesome voice. I was so awestruck hearing your voice when you spoke to me yesterday. By the way, thanks for understanding and respecting my decision, our decision to be precise.

Stephen: No worries, Michelle, thank you, catch up later, bye.

Michelle: Bye, Stephen. *(phone disconnected)*

Chapter 18

Phone ringing...

Stephen: Hello!

Clara: Hi, Sweets, did you send that e-mail to Rachel?

Stephen: Yes, I did...

Clara: And?

Stephen: I am not her type it seems; she says she has changed... it is ok, I am ok. (*silence*)

Clara: You relax, don't worry you will get a nice girl.

Stephen: Really? It doesn't really matter anymore, Clara. I even called my friend Michelle, she also does not want me, even Ziya does not want me, in fact, she refused to even speak to me. They all have become very big...National Award winner, right? She says she does not want to be distracted as she is focusing on her career.

Clara: hmm...it's ok.

Stephen: When did I say I was not ok? I am ok Clara, I am ok with everything, and I respect everyone's decision. Why even you said "no" to me and I respect your decision as well. You all are the same, no one wants me. Ok, Clara... Bye, you sleep. Good night.

Clara: wait...

(I disconnected the phone)

That night was painful, I spoke to myself. I spoke to the one I believe and trust. What did I do so much to be punished so much, my Lord? So much embarrassment... Why?

Daddy had overheard my conversation with Clara and he knew about all the rejections from Michelle and Ziya; he called Clara...

Clara: Hello...

Daddy: Clara, this is Stephen's Daddy.

Clara: Yes, Daddy. *(shocked and puzzled)*

Daddy: Stay away from my, Son, please. I know he loves you a lot; please don't embarrass us in front of the society and our families. Hope you can understand? Hello... Are you listening, Clara?

Clara: Yes, Daddy, I am with you.

Daddy: I know you have helped him a lot and thank you for all that but just stay away from my Son. He is disturbed and is always crying, cannot see my Son like this. He pretends to smile but I know he is in pain.

Clara: But Daddy, that is because...

Daddy: I don't want to hear anything, Clara, just let him live his life peacefully. He is a very sensitive person, and at a very small age he had to take up the burdens of this family because of me. He has gone through a lot, just leave him alone, I don't want to see him hurt anymore because of you or anyone for that matter.

Clara: Ok, but it is quite your fault as well that he is sad. How could you put all your burdens on that little boy? Do you even know what all he has gone through? I know that boy's heart, and I know his pain; every one of you are responsible for his condition.

Daddy: That is our family matter and none of your business.

Clara: Ok not my business, understood... But I have seen him struggle, you could have been a better Father.

Daddy: Stop...enough! (*angry and irritated*) What I have said, I have said... Just stay away from my Son, it is a humble request, please. (*in a stern voice*)

Clara: I am more concerned about him than any of you, I know him well. Trust me, I will never do anything that will affect his life and I will never let him do anything which concerns me that would bring you and your family any shame, you can trust me on that.

Daddy: Thank you, thank you very much; just one more thing... Let this conversation be between us, I don't want him to know about this

Clara: You can trust me on that as well. Ok bye, I need to go. *(phone disconnected)*

Chapter 19

My holidays were over and Clara was not responding to my messages for some reason. She messaged me back in bits and pieces unlike the usual, maybe she was angry that I hung up on her, but she hardly called anymore and even if she picked up my call she was busy and didn't have time to talk. She seemed to be busy always; attitude maybe or maybe she was actually very busy and stressed about work I told to myself. She said she was busy and would not be able to come and pick me up at the airport as well; the day of my return was on a Friday. Why would she be busy on a Friday? No one works on Fridays in UAE or perhaps she was having her periods, but she would have told me that if that was the reason. She is useless in those days. I was all ready to get back to Sharjah the next day; after all the circus and embarrassment and unnecessary tensions. I would be back in my sweetheart's arms, my Clara. I just wanted to kiss her one more time. Why should I be bothered anymore, no more hopes about Rachel, no more hopes about anyone coming into my life anymore? I had made up my mind to have a full-fledged relationship with Clara. I was confident that I could convince her. It was ok if she did not want to get married to me, we would eventually get married someday when she is ready. I wanted to make love to her over and over again, wanted to kiss those beautiful lips, wanted to feel her warm saliva in my mouth, wanted to suck her beautiful nipples for the rest of my life, wanted to live the rest of my life with her.

My bags were packed, and we headed to Kochi airport. I kissed my Daddy and Mummy goodbye. It was an emotional moment for me and for them. Departure or separation was always a difficult moment for me. I was kind of very soft from within, couldn't see anyone cry, I would become emotional on seeing anyone cry, be it anyone for that matter, even if it was a stranger. Clara used to laugh when I used to cry while seeing emotional scenes in the movies. She called me a baby; I was waiting to get back to see another movie with her, lying on her lap, and then Zoyie would push me off her Mom's lap and claim it as her territory, and then we both would sleep on each one of Clara's lap, and then she would run her fingers through my hair.

I sat in the departure lounge thinking of all that had happened during the vacation; about Rachel, Michelle, Ziya, Tina, Ann... I was not angry with any of them. I only had good wishes for them in my heart; but now for some reason, I felt a sense of freedom, I was single and happy, no one was waiting for me and no one wanted me. Everything happens for a reason. *Let God's will be done*, I told myself.

sent an SMS to Clara

Stephen: Are you sure you would not be able to make it to the airport to pick me up?

Clara: No, don't think so, I have some important guests coming home.

Stephen: Shall we see in the evening then? I have brought you banana chips and a few more things.

Clara: That's fine...I don't like banana chips, you can share them with your friends in the room.

Stephen: I want to see you...

Clara: Just leave me alone Stephen, I am busy and quite disturbed with my projects at work, please stay away from me. I need to focus on work or I could lose my job.

Stephen: Are you angry with me or something? What has happened to you?

Clara: I am not fuckin angry, just leave me alone Stephen, please...

Stephen: Why are you abusing? What is happening?

(no response from Clara)

Stephen: When will you be free? When can we meet if not today?

Clara: We will meet when we can. Bye.

Clara had never behaved like this before; it was maybe because she was in a bad mood. She will call me when she is ok but how was I going to go to my accommodation from the Airport. It would cost me a fortune if I was to hire a taxi from the airport. I decided to send Katarina an SMS...

Stephen: Hi Katarina, can you pick me up from the airport if you don't mind and if you are free.

Katarina: Sure when is your flight arrival time?

Stephen: 3:45 PM (UAE time)

Katarina: I will wait for you at the airport.

Stephen: Thank you so much.

Katarina: Don't worry!

Katarina was waiting outside the arrival lounge for me and she came towards me and hugged me as soon as she saw me.

Katarina: I missed you, Stephen.

Stephen: Oh really? How is office?

Katarina: As usual, busy... How was your trip? Parents?

Stephen: The trip was good, parents are fine as well.

Katarina: So how do I look?

Stephen: You look great as usual.

Katarina: Hey, there is a party at my friend's place tonight, you wanna come?

Stephen: No, I just want to rest for some time; just drop me at my accommodation.

Katarina: It is the weekend let's enjoy and the party is at night, it is only 4:30 P.M. now, you can have a shower and rest now and I will come and pick you up at about 9:00 P.M.

Stephen: No, Katarina; I might not be able to make it... you carry on

Katarina: As you wish, I will SMS you before I leave.

Stephen: Yeah, ok!

I reached my cave, at last, my roommates were happy to see me. I shared the Kerala specials with them.

I tried to call Clara, but she didn't answer my call.

I messaged her...

"I reached a few hours back...hope you are fine."

(no reply...)

Something was not right, I told myself. I wanted to go straight to her apartment and ask her what her problem was, and so I decided to SMS Katarina...

Stephen: I need your help, Katarina.

Katarina: Sure, Stephen, tell me...

Stephen: I need to give a few things which I had brought from Kerala to one of my friend; I know you have a party but can you come a little early and pick me up and we will drop this packet at her place and then maybe we could go to the party together?

Katarina: Glad you are coming, sure... I will pick you up by 7:30 P.M.

Stephen: Thank you, Katarina, thank you so much.

Katarina: My pleasure!

Katarina had come to pick me up at the right time, I was all dressed up to see my darling Clara...

Katarina: You look hot, Stephen.

Stephen: Wow, you look awesome as well.

We soon reached below Clara's apartment in the parking lot. I identified Clara's vehicle, so she was there at her place, I messaged her...

Stephen: I am below your apartment...shall I come on top?

Clara: I am not at home!

Stephen: But your car is here.

Clara: Fuck, Stephen! I am not at home, I am at my friend's place.

Stephen: Which friend?

Clara: None of your business... I don't have to tell you everything. Ok...

Stephen: Ok...I will just drop a few things at your place that I have brought for Zoyie.

Clara: No one is in the house and we don't want anything, you can keep it.

Stephen: I am already at the door of your apartment.

Clara: Fuck, Stephen!

I could hear the TV sound from the door, maybe Zoyie was there. I rang the calling bell to Clara's apartment;

no one seemed to open the door and the noise of the TV playing in the background stopped. After a few minutes, I pressed the calling bell once again and the maid opened the door.

Maid: No one is here, Sir.

Stephen: That's ok, just give this to Zoyie baba. (*handing over the bag*)

The maid was hesitant to take the packet and I said, don't worry Clara madam knows.

Maid: Ok, Sir. (*accepting the packet*)

The door closed behind me and after a few seconds I heard Zoyie's voice saying, "*Mumma what is that?*"

I knew that my Clara was inside, but if she didn't want to speak to me then why should I force her, let her take her own time. I went back to Katarina's car and on the way to her party location, I messaged Clara–

Stephen: I know you were in the apartment; I don't know why you are behaving like this but I am sure you have your reasons; we can talk it out if you want.

Clara: Please, Stephen, I don't have the time for this, just leave me alone.

Stephen: Why are you addressing me as "Stephen", you don't usually call me like that.

Clara: Because that is your name…

Stephen: Please, Clara, stop this, I can't take it anymore.

Clara: Just fuck-off, Stephen; just get out of my life.

Stephen: Why? What is wrong with you?

Clara: Don't speak to me as though I owe you something; don't message me anymore and don't try to see me anymore either.

Stephen: What is my fault? Tell me my mistake and I will never bother you again.

(no reply)

We had reached the party spot. I was not in a mood at all, in fact, I was depressed. The party was in one of Katarina's friend's place, the music was thumping and there was food and drinks all around the place. The place was filled with the smell of perfume and cigarette smoke. There were more women on the premises than men. There was a private pool in the back yard and women were in their bikinis laughing, drinking, and playing in the pool.

Katarina: Are you alright, Stephen? Do you want a drink?

Stephen: Yes, please!

Katarina: What would you like to have? Just feel at home, enjoy your self.

Stephen: Anything would do...

After a while, Katarina came to me with her friend and she had a tray full of tequila shots...

Katarina: This is Anna. This is her villa and this is her party. (introducing me to a voluptuous Russian woman)

Anna: Hi.. (*shaking hands with me and placing the other hand on my shoulder*), please feel at home. Here, have a few shots, enjoy yourself. (*chuckles*)

Katarina and I quickly had a few shots and I suddenly started feeling better. There were so many beautiful women in that room and Katarina started taking off her clothes to jump into the pool with her girlfriends.

Katarina was pretty, in fact, all the women in that villa looked extremely attractive; most of them were so naked, and Katarina was hot, her bikini top hardly covered her nipples the rest of her breasts were so much naked and the bottom was a thong which hardly covered her vagina and her buttocks were naked. She was fair and had tiny golden hair all over her body. I could say that she never waxed her body except for her underarms, vaginal area, and her buttocks. She just jumped into the pool (*all the girls giggling and laughing*). Katarina was indicating me to get into the pool with her but I refused. Later she came to me; her nipples were standing out through her bikini top, all wet, wiping her hair with a towel...

Katarina: Hey you alright?

Stephen: Do you have a cigarette?

Katarina: Which brand do you want? We have Marlboro, Davidoff?

Stephen: Marlboro, please.

Katarina: You don't smoke, right?

Stephen: Yeah, just started again.

Katarina: Here take both, try both. (*keeping a packet of each brand on the table along with a lighter*)

Stephen: Thanks!

Katarina: There is food at the other end, you can eat whenever you want and help yourself with whatever you want; enjoy yourself, Stephen.

This was not the first time I was smoking but then I had almost stopped smoking as Clara never liked the smell of smoke, but I had started again, decided to punish myself.

I had a few more shots and kept smoking like a chimney, one after the other, I was feeling hungry and went to the other side to see if there was something to eat, on the way to the other side of the Villa there were rooms, I could hear someone moaning; some were having sex in those rooms. Katarina suddenly came from behind me...

Katarina: Hey come, let's eat something...

Stephen: I think there are people making love in those rooms...

Katarina: The word is sex and not making love. It is normal in our culture, you could bang girls in such parties, except that she should be willing, no rape allowed. Did you like someone here. (*grinning*)

Stephen: Na, not interested.

Katarina: Why? you have a girlfriend already?

Stephen: Na, just broke up with her a few hours back.

Katarina: oh...sorry...that is why you are upset, huh?

Stephen: Life is to enjoy, don't just sulk and sit there; make the first move, go for it enjoy yourself.

We ate some fried chicken some beef rosette along with some pita bread, lamb kebabs, and hummus. By the time the party had finished, it was early morning. Katarina and I were so drunk that we passed out on the couch.

When I woke up there was pin-drop silence; everyone was still sleeping, some were on the floor, some were near the pool area; some were sleeping on the couches; some were literally naked in those bedrooms; there were at least two couples in each bed all naked. It was a sight to see as I had only seen or read about such parties in movies and books, and here I was a part of it today.

I went back to the couch and took up another cigarette, and looked at Katarina's body; she was pretty–a fine tall lady, nothing like what I had ever seen before, she looked like one of those models from the fancy bra and panty ads which come on TV. She opened her eyes slowly. She was waking up as well, and she saw me looking at her nakedness. She slowly raised her head and asked me in a soft husky voice, "What happened, Stephen?"

Stephen: Nothing...

Katarina: You want something? (*smiling*)

Stephen: No! (*smoking*)

Katarina: You want to be laid... (*laughing softly*)

Stephen: What?

Katarina: Want to have sex? (*smiling*)

Stephen: Ah... (*confused and shocked*)

Katarina: Come...

Katarina got up from the couch and caught my hand and walked towards the bedrooms; on seeing that all were utilized she said "Fuck!" (*saying something in Russian*)

Katarina: Can you manage on the floor or on that couch; I am ok with standing also?

Stephen: ah no... It is ok...not now (*refusing and feeling uncomfortable*)

Katarina: You sure?

Stephen: Yeah...but sorry...sorry for not being able to do it now...

Katarina: Hey, no worries... If you want to cum I am ready, that's all I meant; otherwise, for me, it is just normal; it is the guys who have all the fun usually.

Stephen: What do you mean; you never have an orgasm?

Katarina: (*laughing*) Orgasm is a strong word, men just want to bang and once they cum the party is over. I don't even remember the last time I had an orgasm, (grinning)

Stephen: I am sorry!

Katarina: No...never mind, this is very normal for women like me. People think we are very happy, and that we have everything in the world—beauty, designer clothes, expensive perfumes, expensive cars, a good job, lots of money—but all this comes at a price, and that is our sexy bodies which are mostly used by men who provide us with such luxuries. We just have to be ready to get banged and it is only until they cum and we will have to put up with the phrase that "it was good as long as it lasted".

Stephen: I don't see you in that way.

Katarina: I know, I have heard a lot about you, Stephen. You are unlike the other guys who just want to fuck me. You are a nice man. (*hugging me*)

Stephen: Hey, can you drop me at my place? I would like to go home.

Katarina: Sure, just give me two minutes...

Chapter 20

It was raining heavily in UAE, it smelt like home suddenly, dark skies, the sound of thunder. Four years had passed since I spoke to Clara. The last few days with the Sharjah Government as I had resigned, got a better job in Dubai with the Dubai Government.

Lots of changes in my life and around me. It was of the smartphone or we could say the WhatsApp era. I ditched SMSing for good, Facebook and WhatsApp was the thing in life which had now become inevitable. Rachel was married. Michelle and Ziya were also married living their beautiful lives with their families. Tina is my Facebook friend today. We message each other on WhatsApp. She is married as well—she is happy. All my friends are in touch with me—all on WhatsApp and on Facebook. Ann has 2 kids now and Ziya is pregnant with her first; Ziya is a housewife now. It was nice to interact with all of them through Facebook and WhatsApp. No money wasted, all thanks to technology. Clara never replied back to any of my questions or messages, and we never met after that. My interactions with her were limited to messages like "Merry Christmas or Happy New Year" that she never responded to, but thanks to technology, that it informed me that Clara had read my messages; but she was no more the old Clara I knew.

Life moved on, except for my emotions. My emotions were like these raindrops, pouring down with all the might, thundering, yelling with lightning. Only to flow into the drainage or to get absorbed by the desert sand, wasted.

I speak less now, matured a bit more I guess. No more confusions, no more feelings shown on the face. No more tears, got used to all the pain, it was difficult to live without the pain now. Pain has become a part of my life, I liked the pain. Life has changed; I have changed.

Received a WhatsApp message from Ann.

Ann: How are you?

Stephen: Good and you?

Ann: Going on...wish I had fought for us that day with my Appa; he would have said "yes" if I had insisted. I was very young and could never make a decision. Appa was always sad because of his decision; even a few days before his death he mentioned the same.

Stephen: We have discussed all this. Why waste time discussing this over and over again; what has happened now?

Ann: What is to happen more than this? I don't like him...

Stephen: He is your husband; life is like that, you have to adjust. By the way, is it raining there?

Ann: No...why?

Stephen: It is raining here.

Ann: You love the rains, right?

Stephen: Yes!

Ann: When will you be joining your new company?

Stephen: Soon...ok bye...will catch up later...you take care of yourself...bye.

Ann: Yeah...bye.

I decided to go out in the rain. I wanted to have a cup of sulaimani and a samosa, wanted to have a smoke in the rain. I took my car and went out for a drive. I was thankful to this desert, it is like my second home. It gave me everything, it made me what I am today. God might not have heard many of my prayers, but God surely gave me things that I needed most. Respect from everyone, all who had said "no" to me once thought of me highly today. They treated me with respect; the biggest lesson I learnt in life was that money speaks and with money comes respect.

The sulaimani tasted different today, it was raining, the air was cold. I had achieved a lot in these years but I knew from within that I had lost more than I had achieved, but I never stopped praying even though many of my prayers were never answered. I smiled at my Lord above whenever I prayed, we had a connection, a strange connection which no one would understand. I went to the church often not when there was mass but when there was no one in the church. I always felt that I should not be disturbing the Almighty during mass because there would be so many praying to him at that time and he might not be able to concentrate on all their prayer requests, and so I usually went to church when there was no mass, the church would be empty then, it would be just me and my Lord and I could speak to him in person; big people don't reply back, they walk in attitude, and my Lord was the same. He never replied back to me either but he gave me things without me asking for them. What I asked for the most was never granted to me. I had everything today except for myself, I didn't have love within me, I was lonely, I was alone. Someone has rightly said that the greatest pain in this world is to be lonely, alone without love, and loneliness kills slowly but surely.

I parked my car outside the church and walked in, there was silence and it was raining heavily outside. I entered into the silence and I felt warm, it felt as if I was in my territory, protected. I sat in front of the alter for some time. I never prayed that day, I just wanted to sit there for some time. My silence had a lot to say, my Lord must have understood, no one else would or even cared to understand.

It was my last day at work with the Sharjah Government, it was my farewell day. There was a small party organized in my Department. I sat on my chair for the last few hours before I departed to a new place. There were a lot of good words showered upon me. I remembered Hassan Ikka. I remembered the 20 dirhams in my pocket and the night I had got out of my sister's place. I remembered me stealing water and I remembered the smelly food I had to eat as dinner in those days as I had nothing else to eat other than the leftovers from the afternoon packed lunch. Many had come along to bid me farewell; but I missed Clara, my Clara, who had stood by me when I was a nobody. The one who made me a man. She was the first woman I had ever touched. It was raining outside. While everyone was enjoying the good food, I was looking out of the window watching the rain. I was quiet, remembering some of the good and bad times until that point of my life, Katarina came up to me.

Katrina: It was an honor to work with you.

Stephen: It was nice knowing you Katarina, please keep in touch.

Katarina: Sure, Sir! Can I tell you something?

Stephen: Sure, go ahead...

Katarina: Thank you for everything. I never thought I would ever tell a man something like this but you are different Stephen. Every man who I have met until now only wanted to use me, but you are the only one who never touched me, even though you had many chances you never even attempted once. What are you, man? I was always off guard when I was with you, but you were always a gentleman, never once did you make an attempt.

Stephen: Really? I never knew you were off guard (*laughing*). All the best, Katarina, take care of yourself. See you sometime... Keep in touch and thank you for everything. (*shaking hands*).

The office boy brought me my favorite drink one last time–Sulaimani with Saffron and Rose Water.

After thanking everyone and my office boy for one last time, I left the office who made me what I was today. I was in peace, happy. It was still raining, and the wind was cold.

Chapter 21

I was introduced to my new Manager by HR.

HR: This is Stephen and Stephen this is your Manager, Bethany

Stephen: Hi, Bethany.

Bethany: Hi, Stephen, welcome to our department.

Bethany was from the UK, she was not a pleasant woman, she was abusive, loud, and always found a reason to fight with everyone. I was happy with my new organization but this woman, my Manager, was a headache. She literally used to keep me under the microscope, and it was difficult to work with her. It used to be always her way and I was not allowed to do anything independently.

Months passed by and life moved on when I received a message on WhatsApp.

Michelle: Hi, there.

Stephen: Hi, Michelle.

Michelle: I am in Dubai.

Stephen: Oh really? Where?

Michelle: I am at the Media Palace Hotel, it's a two-day business trip.

Stephen: Good, can we meet?

Michelle: Sure, was going to ask you actually.

Stephen: Are you free at about 6:30 P.M. today, I could pass by after work then?

Michelle: No, not today. I am at this seminar the whole day today and I am not sure when this would end.

Stephen: Oh...ok...

Michelle: Can we meet tomorrow?

Stephen: Sure, at what time?

Michelle: I will be busy all afternoon, but will be free in the evening.

Stephen: I will pass by at about 6:30 P.M. then.

Michelle: Yeah ok...but don't be late...I have a flight to catch.

Stephen: When is your flight?

Michelle: It is at about 12:30 A.M. I will have to check out from the hotel at about 10:00 P.M.

Stephen: I will be there by 6:30 P.M.

Michelle: Cool ok...see you tomorrow then...bye!

Stephen: Bye!

It was after almost 15 years that I was going to see Michelle, I have seen her photos pop up on Facebook but the thought of seeing her in person was a different feeling.

I parked my car in the parking area of the hotel where Michelle was staying and I quickly picked up my phone and sent her a message.

Stephen: I am here!

Michelle: I am at the café inside the hotel.

Stephen: Yeah, coming.

Michelle was sitting there on one of the tables waiting for me. Michelle was excited to see me and she got up and hugged me.

Michelle: Oh my God, you look so handsome, Stephen.

Stephen: Thanks...

Michelle: How are you?

Stephen: I am good, going on; how about you?

Michelle: Yeah...all well, so happy to see you, Stephen, can't believe my eyes. (*blushing*)

Stephen: It's been almost 15 years that we have met right?

Michelle: 16 years, Stephen, I am glad that you came. (*blushing*)

Stephen: you have changed a lot Michelle; I still remember that beautiful girl in her school uniform... your phone calls and our conversations (*giggles*)

Michelle: Those were the best days of my life, Stephen, I will never be able to forget the time spent with you. Why are you not married yet?

Stephen: You never accepted my proposal right? (*laughing*)

Michelle: Really? (*blushing*) So tell me, are you seeing someone? I mean do you have a girlfriend, an affair?

Stephen: Nope, nothing like that; how many kids do you have. (*trying to change the topic*)

Michelle: Trying to change the topic huh. (*smiling*) I have two kids, two boys.

Stephen: Nice... How is Ziya? Do you guys meet?

Michelle: Ziya is fine, she and her husband have started a coaching center for kids, they are happily settled except that she could not qualify for the Olympics last time, it was her dream actually.

Stephen: she can try again right, what is there to get upset about?

Michelle: No, Stephen, she is a married woman now, and even though her husband's family is supportive she has to fulfill the duties of a wife, of a daughter-in-law, and take care of the house, and so she decided to give it up. She helps her husband at the coaching center.

Stephen: That's sad, she should have given it one more shot.

Michelle: Do you guys not WhatsApp each other?

Stephen: Yes we do, a "hi" and "bye" now and then...

Michelle: To be honest we both liked you a lot. (*holding my hand...blushing*)

Stephen: Hey, shall we go out for dinner? (*changing the topic*)

Michelle: No, I will just have a sandwich, I don't eat much when I have to fly, I have gastric issues. Oh by the way sorry, what would you like to have?

Stephen: Just a cappuccino.

Michelle: Don't worry, order whatever you want. I am not paying for it from my pocket it is all on my company. (*laughing*)

Stephen: No, I only want a cappuccino.

Michelle ordered two cappuccinos and a chicken club sandwich; we ate and drank and then I decided to leave.

Stephen: So...shall I leave now?

Michelle: What is the hurry, help me pack my bags, come with me.

Michelle took me to her room. It was a decent room, well-furnished, there were lots of clothes lying over here and there and a few shopping bags filled with chocolates and biscuits, etc. which she had bought for her kids.

Michelle: Hey, can you please help me pack all this I am very bad at packing; I will just have a quick shower and come back.

Stephen: Sure!

I started packing all her clothes one by one; there were used clothes in one corner and so I decided to pack them separately without mixing them with the fresh ones. I emptied one of the shopping bags and arranged all the dirty clothes in them folding them one after the other, her used undergarments were beneath among them. I looked at them and smiled, how I had wanted to see her breast in our school days. Her breasts were her highlights, and here I was today alone with her in a hotel room, holding her bra and panty in my hands which smelled of her sweat, and here she was naked in the bathroom having a shower just a few feet away from me. I packed all her clothes as instructed, fresh clothes, chocolates and biscuits in one bag and her used clothes in another bag. There were still more to pack but then I left that to her as she would surely have a last-minute packing as she would want to use a few things to get dressed. Michelle came out of the bathroom in a towel robe provided by the hotel.

Michelle: Wow, you are good at this man...nice, I am impressed. *(her eyes were looking for something...)* There were some clothes here, where is that?

Stephen: Ah the used ones, I kept them in this bag.

Michelle: My undergarments were there. *(blushing)*

Stephen: I have safely packed it, don't worry.

Michelle: No not that, I was planning to wear them now. The one I was wearing all this while is sweaty and wet; the one you packed might have dried up by now. I just brought 2 pairs with me... (*blushing*) Short trip, right!

Stephen: Ok wait. (*got her undergarments for her from her bag*) Here...give me the ones in your hand I will keep it inside.

Michelle: No... It is ok, I will pack it. (*blushing*)

I just grabbed them from her and packed them for her

Stephen: Everything is packed except for your make-up set, you can do that once you are done; so shall I go now? It is already 9:00 P.M., you will have to leave by 10:00 P.M. right.

Michelle: Yeah, ok...thanks for coming Stephen, and thank you for all the help. (*blushing*)

Stephen: No worries, take care of yourself, and keep in touch.

Michelle quickly came close to me and hugged me, her whole body weight was on me suddenly and she lifted up her head and kissed my lips. I was shocked by her gesture. She pushed me towards the wall and kissed me even harder now. She opened her robe and she was naked inside; her nipples were big and her breasts were huge, hanging, but they looked beautiful, her body emitted the smell of the shower gel she had just used. Her flabby tummy was hanging covering her abdomen; she had stretch marks on her stomach from her pregnancy but her stretch marks looked beautiful. I hugged her naked body pressing it to mine and she sighed in content. She looked at my eyes and said, "I have dreamt of this moment a thousand times dear."

I told to myself that I had dreamt to see your breasts in our school days as well, and here she was today naked in my arms.

She hungrily kissed me and started removing the belt from my pants trying to unhook my pants, but I pushed her off and said "no...please...". She kept kissing me and placed my hands on her naked breasts probing me to squeeze them and make love to her, but for some reason my mind refused, I didn't want to, and she understood that I was hesitant and so she stopped and asked–

"I am not beautiful enough for you now, right? I forgot for a moment that you are not the old Stephen anymore." (*teasing*)

Stephen: No my dear, I have always dreamt of your body; it's just that I am tired, not in a mood, sorry.

Michelle: Ok! (*smiling*)

Michelle took her undergarments from the bed and started putting them on. She indicated me to put on the hooks to her bra, I walked behind her and put them on for her. She quickly put on her panties and got dressed.

Stephen: Hey, you angry with me?

Michelle: No...not at all, don't be silly. (*smiling*)

Stephen: I am sorry, I just can't, it is not because you are not beautiful or anything, your breasts are the best I have ever seen, you have a beautiful body as well, it's just me, my mind.

Michelle: I really loved you a lot, Stephen. I was stupid to say "no" to you; I was more bothered about my friendship with Ziya and now when I think all of that was bullshit. (*laughing*)

Stephen: Are you not happy with your marriage?

Michelle: oh yes, I am happy (*being sarcastic*), marriage is a drama, Stephen, (*smiling*) first you get married and then the acting starts, then you have secrets and then you have to hide those secrets (*laughing*), full acting (*smiling*). I loved you a lot Stephen and I am sorry if I have ever hurt you, forgive me if possible. (*eyes filled with tears*)

Stephen: No, my dear, I am not at all angry with you; just be happy, don't worry, everything will be fine

Michelle just hugged me once again and kissed my lips and she smiled and said, "I will never be able to forget you". After saying that she kissed me once again on my lips. (*tears flowed from her eyes*) I held her face in my hands and looking into her eyes kissed her forehead and said to her "God Bless you my dear" (*tears rolled down my cheeks*). Michelle immediately wiped my tears with her hands and said, "Men don't cry." (*trying to smile, tears rolling down her cheeks*).

After a few minutes, I bid her farewell and left the room.

Later I received a message from Michelle saying that she had reached India safely and that she would never ever forget the night with me in that hotel room.

Chapter 22

Stephen: Planning to go to Kerala to see my parents; Mummy had a stroke recently, by God's Grace it was detected at the right time and immediately she was shifted to a medical facility. She is much better, but I want to see my parents. Bethany, I would like to go on annual leave...

Bethany: Sure, just apply for it and I will approve; how many days are you planning for?

Stephen: 15 days...

Bethany: Yeah sure, go ahead and apply.

So I booked my tickets to go to Kerala, Kochi, going on vacation was always fun but this time it was to see my Mummy.

Whenever I think of Mummy what comes into my mind was the days when I was very young going to a school in Calcutta; my Daddy in those days had a small printing and offset business set up adjacent to my home. Daddy was quite an influential person, and everyone respected him. There were so many of my cousins who were brought down from Kerala so that they could get a good education and life at the expense of my parents. For Daddy, it was supposed to be saving lives or making a career for all these young people in his family back in Kerala. Now there was this municipality tap in our backyard which was connected to the water tank outside the house. At that time, we never had a water pump in our house to pump this water from the tank outside our house to fill the tank inside our bathroom. I remember Mummy carrying buckets of water in both her hands to fill the tank inside our bathroom so that all the people residing in our home (about 16 people including herself) could have a bath, use the toilet, etc.; she used to carry water to wash clothes as well in the same way.

I remember Mummy washing all of their clothes, we never had a washing machine, there was a small stone kept on the floor of the bathroom; she literally had to kneel in the bathroom to get all these clothes washed. All of these cousins never even offered to help, they only threw their dirty clothes in the corner including their undergarments. There was not a single day that she didn't have anything to wash; I remember seeing her drenched in soap water; she used to be wet from top to bottom, in sweat, water, and dirt.

She used to rush to collect me and my sister from our schools after all that work in that same saree. To see my Mummy at school meant that she would buy me and my sister an ice cream. She used to hang both our school bags on both her shoulders and walk while we ate the tasty ice cream she had bought us.

Then she would have to rush back home to make the rest of the curries and dishes for lunch for these 16 people in the house, at times, there would be uninvited guests (Daddy's friends). The food service in our house was great, bed coffee for everyone in the house, breakfast for everyone in the house; for some breakfast had to be packed and some would have from my home; then lunch in the afternoon; tea and snacks for everyone in the evening and dinner for everyone as well. Can you imagine the amount of food my Mummy had to cook all by herself? The amount of dishes she had to wash after every meal? I was too small then to question my Daddy.

My Mummy always had a smile on her face even after all this. There were days when she had no food to eat due to the uninvited guests as she might have had to serve them her share of the meal. I am sure the poor thing went hungry many times and no one ever cared.

Today my Mummy is unwell, she is probably worn out; I feel she has done all the work a human being could do in a lifetime by now, and her body required rest.

Mummy means love to me, Mummy means sacrifice to me, Mummy means tasty good food to me. She loved us so much and she would do anything for us.

I reached Kerala to see my Mummy and the first thing, as usual, was her tears and hugs and her kisses. My Mummy was safe, feeling better. She was alone in that house with my Daddy in Kerala. No one for whom Daddy had made careers or had sponsored offered to help; no one came in to see the poor women who had washed their clothes; no one paid a visit to the sick and tired women who had made good and tasty food for them when they were hungry. Not a single person went hungry even if Mummy had to sleep without eating anything for dinner. She made sure that we all were full and content before she even looked inside those vessels to see if there was anything left for her to eat.

I sat with my Mummy for a long time that day. I was happy to see her again, I was happy that she was resting, I was happy that she was still smiling at me without any complaints as ever.

I received a WhatsApp message on my phone...

Rachel: I reached Bangalore a couple of days back; this is my number please message me when you are free.

Stephen: Hi Rachel, just reached here a few hours back.

Rachel: How is your Mummy?

Stephen: She is fine by God's Grace, she is happy to see me.

Rachel: Hey, I will be going to Delhi for a couple of days; why don't you also come.

Stephen: Delhi...why?

Rachel: Nothing, just to unwind a bit.

Stephen: How about your baby?

Rachel: My parents are here and they will look after her.

Stephen: Let's see, I am not sure, I prefer staying with my Mummy. I want to be by her side.

Rachel: It is only for a couple of days; try to come if possible.

Stephen: Yeah, let me see... When are you planning to leave?

Rachel: Tomorrow afternoon.

Stephen: And when are you planning to return to Canada?

Rachel: I will be here for a month and then my husband would come and then we all would return to Canada together.

Stephen: Ok... I will let you know Rachel.

Rachel: I will message you later, Stephen, my husband is calling.

Stephen: Yeah sure, bye.

Rachel: Bye!

That night I spoke to Mummy and Daddy a lot, they just wanted me to get married. Mummy was worried that she would not be able to see her grandchildren before her death. Daddy inquired about Clara and I said that we hardly speak anymore, I saw a sense of relief on my father's face at my answer. We had dinner together.

 I called Rachel at night.

Rachel: Hello!

Stephen: Hi, Stephen.

Rachel: Oh hi, is this your India number?

Stephen: Yes!

Rachel: Had dinner?

Stephen: Yes, and you?

Rachel: Yes... I had dinner; hey I sent you a picture on your WhatsApp, have a look...

Stephen: Yeah sure!

Rachel: Have a look at it now, and see if you can recognize that person.

Stephen: Ahh! Our farewell day photo; how can I ever forget you in that saree, how can I ever forget that night.

Rachel: Do you recognize that second picture?

Stephen: What is this?

Rachel: These are the same old earrings that you bought me.

Stephen: Oh my God! (astonished and shocked) Do you still have them?

Rachel: Of course, I loved them a lot and I will keep them with me forever

Stephen: Can I ask you something!

Rachel: Sure...shoot!

Stephen: Why did you say "no" to me?

Rachel: By the time you had sent me that e-mail my guy had already asked my parents for my hand, you were slightly late

Stephen: hmm

Rachel: See if you can make it to Delhi.

Stephen: I would not be able to make it Rachel; I will try to come to Bangalore before I leave India; you enjoy your trip

Rachel: Yeah ok; hey but don't expect anything much when you see me ok. (*grinning*)

Stephen: No expectations at all, so don't worry.

Rachel: So what else?

Stephen: Nothing, I was just thinking, years back I used to wish if I had a chance to speak to you like this, everything seems to be a miracle now...

And then I told Rachel, how I used to pray to the Lord for her, I told her about the myth that I believed in about going to churches and praying for her. I told her about the way I was molested on that bus. The pains I took to chat with her on MSN, to which Rachel replied...

Rachel: You should have told me Stephen; everyone else in school knew that you loved me except for me, you should have told me at least once...

The normal rubbishing which all the girls say, I told to myself

Stephen: Ok then Rachel, catch up later...good night.

Rachel: I will call you tomorrow, bye, good night.

Stephen: Bye, good night.

The next day Rachel sent me a selfie of herself just about to board the Delhi flight, and I thought to myself that life is strange, and how priorities changed with time; there was a time when I wished if I could see Rachel. I used to blame the distance and the technology then for not being able to see her; today I had everything, be it money, technology, or be it anything for that matter and the best part was that she was in India, and still, I was not able to meet her, or maybe I didn't want to see her, or maybe it was not meant to be.

I was shocked to see those earrings; it was with her even today. I was happy to know that she thought of me, maybe she had some kind of feelings for me; there was no point in thinking about old things and I had to move on and I told myself that as long as she is happy what more did I ever want, may God Bless her and her family.

Phone ringing...

Rachel: Hello, Stephen.

Stephen: Hi!

Rachel: I have just boarded the flight.

Stephen: Yeah, let me know if you need anything and take care of yourself.

Rachel: Yeah sure!

Stephen: And don't expect much from our friends there in Delhi; people change.

Rachel: I know, Stephen, I will message you from there, and do let me know if at all you change your mind and decide to come. (*giggles*)

Stephen: Yeah sure, but it is quite unlikely; I will try to come and see you in Bangalore when you are back.

Rachel: Yeah sure!

Stephen: Hope your parents would not mind; anyway, I will come prepared. (*laughing*)

Rachel: Na... Don't worry they are harmless. (*giggles*)

Stephen: So, have a safe journey and call me if you need anything; don't hesitate.

Rachel: Sure, I will... bye.

Stephen: Bye, Rachel!

Rachel: Bye!

Chapter 23

Stephen: Daddy are you sure you want a car now, I mean now?

Daddy: Yes, I want one before you go back.

Stephen: Ok then, let me know what you are looking for and if I find it feasible I will get it for you.

Daddy: A second hand one would also do, but we need a car here or else we will have to keep hearing that question over and over again.

Stephen: What question?

Daddy: Which car do you have? Apparently, the status of a person is judged by the vehicle they use. Whenever we go to visit a potential bride for you we keep facing this question, so this time get us a car before you go.

Stephen: Yeah ok, but I am not coming with you guys to see any potential bride this time, let Mummy recover completely first and then we will think about my marriage.

Mummy: I am getting old my Son and so is your Daddy; we would like to see you settled down and happy before our time comes.

Stephen: Ah don't worry, Mummy, you both won't die any time soon. (*laughing*) There is a long way to go for both of you.

Daddy: There is this nice girl, she is a relative of one of my friend; why don't we meet her before you leave.

Stephen: No, Daddy, not this time, I want to be at peace this time, I want to relax.

Daddy: Do you have someone in mind already? Tell us if that is the case and then we don't have to waste our time

Stephen: No, Daddy, nothing like that; it is just that I am not interested; can we talk about something else please (*wanting to change the topic*); so which car do you want?

Daddy: Nothing fancy... A Suzuki Baleno would do

Stephen: Are you sure, why don't you opt for a bigger car?

Daddy: I need to be comfortable driving it; Baleno is small and easy to handle, but I want an automatic gear model.

Stephen: You mean automatic transmission?

Daddy: Yes!

Stephen: Ok, let's go visit the showroom tomorrow itself.

Daddy: Sure, ok; by the way who were you speaking to a while back?

Stephen: Who? Rachel?

Daddy: Rachel is that same girl from your school days right?

Stephen: Yes...

Daddy: Do you like each other even now?

Stephen: She is married, Daddy, she has a kid as well; she is in India now for vacation and that's why she called.

Later that day Daddy made a few calls to the Suzuki showroom in Kochi and he was convinced that Baleno was what he wanted. We were asked to pay an advance for the booking of the vehicle at the earliest.

So I asked Daddy to go and pay some advance.

Daddy: Are you not coming with me?

Stephen: Mummy will be alone here Daddy, I would prefer being with her.

Daddy: I don't feel like going alone.

Stephen: I will ask Shinoy to accompany you.

The next day morning Daddy and Shinoy went to the Suzuki showroom and paid the advance, and Daddy requested the salesman there that he required the delivery of the vehicle in two weeks and the salesman asked them to speak to the Branch Manager. The salesman immediately guided them to the branch manager's cabin. The Branch Manager introduced herself....

"I am Caren. How may I help you? Please have a seat..."

Shinoy: I have seen you somewhere?

Caren: Aren't you Stephen's cousin... Forgot your name though...

Shinoy: I am Shinoy...

Caren: Hi, Shinoy, what a surprise!

Shinoy: Yeah (laughing). I never knew you were the Branch Manager here; well, this is Stephen's Daddy...

Caren: (*standing up from her seat*) Hello, Daddy, how is Stephen? Where is he?

Daddy: Stephen is working in Dubai now, but he has come for his vacation; he will be here until the end of this month; so how do you know each other?

Caren: We all were in college together.

Daddy: So you are Caren. (*smiling*)

Caren: Yes, Daddy, I am that Caren. (*smiling*)

Daddy: So you married?

Caren: Yes.

Daddy: Kids?

Caren: Yes, one...daughter. How about Stephen?

Daddy: No, he is not married yet, we are looking for a bride for him actually.

Caren: Oh...ok; how about you Shinoy?

Shinoy: I am married; a baby is on the way. (*laughing*)

Caren: Congratulations...

Shinoy: Thanks

Caren: So how may I help you?

Daddy: We just paid some advance to get the boooking done for a vehicle; Stephen will be here in India only for another 2 weeks and it would be very helpful if we could get the vehicle as soon as possible before he leaves

Caren: Daddy, can I have a look at the receipt please? *(looking into her system to verify the details)* So you have opted for a Baleno, full options, automatic drive, pearl white and you are going to pay in cash.

Daddy: That's right, cash or current dated cheque.

Caren picked up her phone and called her logistics team...

Caren: What is the status of the vehicle for Mr. Stephen? customer number 104109?

Logistics team representative: We have just booked it, Ma'am.

Caren: When do you think this vehicle would be ready for delivery?

Logistics team representative: At least two weeks, Ma'am, and then a couple of days for preparation of the vehicle and then one day for the registration process.

Caren: Can this vehicle be delivered now?

Logistics team representative: Now?

Caren: I mean today or by tomorrow?

Logistics team representative: No way Ma'am; we will only get the consignment in two weeks.

Caren: ok, I will tell you what, I can see a full option vehicle, exactly with all the options we are looking for in the system; please get that vehicle ready for registration today itself and the delivery should be done by tomorrow.

Logistics team representative: But Ma'am, that is a limited edition vehicle anniversary model; which is kept reserved for VIPs just in case we have an immediate requirement

Caren: Well this is for a VIP; so make it fast; bring in the invoice to me ASAP.

Logistics team representative: Sure, Ma'am. (*phone disconnected*)

Caren: Daddy you will get the delivery of the vehicle tomorrow; they will bring the invoice now and you can make the payment; if you are not prepared now for the payment you can very well pay it tomorrow at the time of delivery.

Daddy: That was quick!

Caren: Anything for Stephen's Daddy. (*smiling*)

Daddy quickly called me...

Stephen: Yes Daddy, everything alright?

Daddy: We will get the vehicle tomorrow itself?

Stephen: What? Are you sure?

Daddy: Your friend is here, Caren, she is the Branch Manager here; Wait I will give the phone to Shinoy, I have a few documents to sign.

Stephen: Ok!

Shinoy: Bhai, Caren is here... B.Com...understood? (*grinning*) She arranged a limited-edition vehicle for us and that too at a discounted price, cheaper than what was told to us earlier; she has also agreed to give all the accessories free of cost including the seat covers. Do you want to speak to her?

Stephen: Where is she?

Shinoy: She is with Daddy helping him complete all the formalities for the Registration; hopefully the formalities will be completed today itself and they will deliver the vehicle by tomorrow morning or by afternoon.

Stephen: Can I speak to her?

Shinoy: Bhai, she is married, has one daughter also.

Stephen: Give her the phone, please...

Shinoy: Sure! (*handing over the phone to Caren...it is Stephen, he wants to speak to you*)

Caren: Hi, Stephen!

Stephen: Hey...hi, what a surprise!

Caren: Oh my gosh, I can't believe I am speaking to you... It's been so many years.

Stephen: Yeah...hey thanks for all your help; you made this happen so fast, thank you so much.

Caren: Anything for you, Stephen.

Stephen: Thanks for the discount as well and all the free stuff. Daddy and Shinoy told me...

Caren: Ah don't thank me; I am just doing my job.

Stephen: When will I get the delivery?

Caren: Late by tomorrow afternoon, but should be ready by morning itself, by 11:00 A.M.

Stephen: Ok, can I send a cheque through Daddy for the total outstanding amount?

Caren: No, we would require a demand draft, I will WhatsApp you the bank details, and then you can ask your bank to prepare it for you.

Stephen: Sure ok, you can give the bank details to Daddy.

Caren: Why? Give me your mobile number? (*grinning*)

Stephen: Sure, take it from Shinoy, it is the same number we are speaking right now; to be honest, I don't remember it by heart myself (*laughing*), I use this number only when I am in India.

Caren: Sure, I will take it from him; you will be coming to take the delivery tomorrow right?

Stephen: I will try; actually Mummy is not keeping well so someone needs to be here with her.

Caren: Yeah...Daddy told me about Mummy; don't bother if you cannot make it tomorrow I will come to your place and see you before you go back; I can see Mummy also then.

Stephen: Just do everything that is required for Daddy ok.

Caren: Don't worry, I have got this Stephen, I will handle everything, you relax and stay calm. So what else?

Stephen: Nothing, just going on.

Caren: Why are you not married yet?

Stephen: Maybe because I don't have a car; at least, that is what my Daddy thinks. *(laughs)*

Caren: No Stephen, on a serious note, why?

Stephen: Nothing like that, just that it did not happen, that's it.

Caren: is it because of me? *(in a very low voice)*

Stephen: Hey, not at all; you are married right?

Caren: I have a daughter as well.

Stephen: Same guy?

Caren: Yeah...Robin; let me help Daddy finish these formalities.

Stephen: Sure, go on and thank you once again.

Caren: I don't want any of your thank you. *(laughing)* I want to see you, you need to buy me lunch. *(laughing)*

Stephen: Sure... I will, bye.

Caren: Bye *(phone disconnected)*

That evening all the vehicle formalities were done and Daddy was so happy that he was getting a new vehicle and that too in record time.

WhatsApp message from Rachel...

Rachel: Hi, how are you?

Stephen: I am good, how are you? All well? Enjoying?

Rachel: All good! I am literally having a blast; you should have been here.

Stephen: hmm...hey I am buying a car for Daddy.

Rachel: What? Car?

Stephen: Yeah, why what happened?

Rachel: I mean you are telling me you are buying a car like as though you are buying a chocolate.

Stephen: No, we don't have a car right now; after Daddy's business fell apart, we had to sell everything and then we never bought another vehicle; so he needed one and that's why...

Rachel: Cool, nice... You are a really good person and a good Son.

Stephen: Hey, nothing like that, I am just doing whatever is necessary for my family. So when are you returning?

Rachel: The day after tomorrow, the morning flight to Bangalore.

Stephen: Ok, had dinner?

Rachel: Yeah, just finished.

Stephen: Did you take any pictures?

Rachel: No pictures! (LOL)

Stephen: Yeah ok, enjoy. (LOL)

Rachel: I will message you later, bye.

Stephen: Yeah sure, bye.

Phone ringing...call from Caren...

Caren: Hi, Stephen...

Stephen: Hi, Caren. I will go to the bank tomorrow and get the DD as per your Performa Invoice and I will send it through Daddy or I will come in myself.

Caren: Yeah sure; your registration has been completed; they have started preparing the vehicle and it will be ready by morning itself hopefully.

Stephen: Thanks Caren for everything.

Caren: What thanks Stephen; at least let me do this for you; I still feel guilty about us.

Stephen: Leave all that; why dig up an old grave.

Caren: No, Stephen, you should know a few things; it was only recently that Robin told me about the call he had made to you after you had spoken to me that day; in fact, I was wondering why you did not call me ever again after that night.

Stephen: Caren, you must have given my number to Robin and might have told him everything otherwise how would he know that I had called you and why would he get so angry; moreover, I did ask you many times if you both liked each other and you kept saying there was nothing between you both. (*laughing*)

Caren: I can explain, Stephen... When you had called Robin was here in my house, we were studying together, and he was listening to our conversation; he might have called you after that; I was not aware of that call.

Stephen: How did he get my number then?

Caren: I have no idea.

Stephen: He called me almost immediately after I had disconnected your call.

Caren: Whatever it is you should have called me back, Stephen.

Stephen: I felt cheated and I did not feel like calling you after that.

Caren: I am innocent in this, trust me; I was not having any kind of relationship with Robin, we were good friends and that's it but I never knew he loved me and I never knew he had called until a few months back when he confessed to me. Stephen, if you had called me once after that then things might have been different today.

Stephen: Hey, leave all that, Caren; as long as you are happy, I am happy, what else do I need.

Caren: No, Stephen, please trust me I never knew all this had happened.

Stephen: I trust you, don't worry. (*laughing*)

Caren: Robin has done this to many guys who were interested in me, it was not just with you; I was ok to marry any person as long as my parents were ok with it; in fact, my parents knew about you; I wish you had called me one more time.

Stephen: Are you not happy?

Caren: Happy is a strong word Stephen; I am fine, going on. I have a daughter and she is my life.

Stephen: Doesn't he take care of you?

Caren: He is a good man; to be honest, he deserves an award for tolerating me, it is just that I feel empty from within; I keep looking for someone in the crowd; maybe it is your curse.

Stephen: I have not cursed anyone (*laughing*), and will never do that ever. It is true that I felt very bad and cried, but I can never curse you.

Caren: Your tears... That might be the reason for my emptiness.

Stephen: What is gone wrong with you Caren, we were kids then, just relax; your life is perfect, and Robin is a nice and handsome guy. I am nowhere close to him. You have got the best, trust me. I was never a match for a woman like you. Forget about all this and sleep; I will try to come down to the showroom to take the delivery tomorrow.

Caren: Why are you not married even now?

Stephen: No, nothing, I had responsibilities so was busy with that; it is not that I do not want to get married or anything; it is just that I have not found the right girl yet. My marriage will happen when it is time.

Caren: I really feel guilty when I see you not settled with a family until now.

Stephen: You don't have to my dear; be sure that me being single until now has nothing to do with you; when it is time I will surely get married, I don't intend to be a bachelor all my life.

Caren: I am not a cheat, please don't think of me that way. (*sad tone*)

Stephen: Caren, go sleep! (*laughing*) I will see you tomorrow. Bye, good night.

Caren: ok...bye. (*sad tone*)

That was a night that I could never forget. I had two women contacting me who had played important roles in my life—one was my love from school days and the other from my college days and I thought to myself that something was missing. Clara was missing, and I decided to send Clara a WhatsApp message.

Stephen: Hi, Clara.

Clara: Hi, how are you?

Stephen: I am fine and you?

Clara: Good, thank you.

Stephen: I am in India, flew in for a couple of weeks, Mummy is not well.

Clara: What happened to Mummy?

Stephen: She had a stroke, but she is fine now, recovering.

Clara: Oh that's sad; hope she feels better.

Stephen: How is Zoyie?

Clara: She is fine, she has become a big girl now.

Stephen: Can I ask you something?

Clara: Sure!

Stephen: What happened between us?

(no reply from the other end)

Stephen: I have asked you this so many times. It's been quite long now and I would like to know. It was after one of the holidays that you started acting weird. Fair enough you have your own reasons for not being able to marry me and I respect your feelings and I will never ever force you to marry me, it is just that I need my old friend back. It's been so many years now, and I am sorry if I have hurt you in any way, sorry if I have done anything wrong to you, but please, I need you, I need my best friend.

(after a couple of minutes)

Clara: Don't be upset, it is me who is crazy. I wanted to keep a distance from you and it was for your own good; you deserve someone better.

Stephen: Can I call you? It's been so many years that we have talked, please.

Clara: I will call you, but where are you now?

Stephen: At my home where else?

Clara: No, I meant where in your home?

Stephen: In my room, why?

Clara: Are your parents anywhere close by?

Stephen: No, but why are you asking all this?

Clara: Nothing, just like that; just make sure your door is closed, and nobody can hear us. I will call you in two minutes.

Stephen: Yeah, ok.

Phone ringing

Stephen: Hello!

Clara: Hi!

Stephen: What is wrong with you, we are not school kids, what if my parents hear our conversation.

Clara: Chill, relax, it's just that I don't want any trouble.

Stephen: What trouble? Hang on...did my parents tell you anything?

Clara: (*silence for a couple of seconds*) No, nothing.

Stephen: Clara, tell me the truth.

Clara: No man, nothing. (*almost crying*)

Stephen: Tell me, what did they tell you?

Clara: Nothing man, just leave it. (*crying*)

Stephen: Why are you crying, my dear?

Clara: Don't ask me anything, I don't want to speak about it, I will hang up if you ask me anymore.

Stephen: Thank you for calling me.

Clara: I don't want your 'thank you'. (*giggling, trying to stop crying*)

In the background can hear Zoyie consoling her mother "Ma, why are you crying?; please don't cry, or I will also cry." Clara: Ma is not crying you don't worry.

Stephen: Stop crying, please...

Clara: I am not, I am fine.

Stephen: So what else?

Clara: You tell me?

Then we spoke about quite a lot of things. I told her everything that had happened in my life until then. I told her about my new job, Rachel, Ann, Caren, Michelle, Ziya, and the call lasted for about 2 hours.

Clara: So, you have become a stud now, huh?

Stephen: No, nothing like that. (*giggling*)

I suddenly felt much younger, I felt as though I got back my life

Clara: How is Mummy? Is she fine?

Stephen: She is alright; she will recover but it is going to take some time. She is fine.

Clara: I am very proud of you sweetheart.

Stephen: Wow... I had been waiting for years to hear you call me that.

Clara: What? Sweetheart? (*giggling*)

Stephen: Yeah, it is like oxygen to me... You won't understand it.

Clara: Yeah... yeah, I don't understand anything now, you have so many other women to understand your feelings now isn't it. (*giggling*)

Stephen: I hope I could show you how much I love you.

Clara: I know my dear. I know you very well, but I am so happy for you, you have grown up to be a strong man. You finished all your responsibilities, and now you are gifting a car to your parents. Wow... I could never do any of what you are doing now for my parents. I am so proud of you, and I am very happy to have called you today. It is too late now; go to bed, sleep.

Stephen: Yes, Madam. (*giggling*)

Clara: And you call me next time, I am not as rich as you are. (*laughing*)

Stephen: Sure, I will.

Clara: Bye, good night.

Stephen: Bye, good night and love you...

Clara: Hmm...

Stephen: Bye! (*giggling*) Will call you tomorrow.

Clara: Yeah ok, but call me when you are alone, please...

Stephen: Yeah ok, understood. Bye.

Clara: Bye! (*phone disconnected*)

Mummy: I want to tell you something, but promise me that you won't get upset or get angry.

Mummy: Tell me, I am listening.

Stephen: Mummy, I love Clara. I love her a lot, and I want to marry her. I know she is very much elder to me but I feel she is the right person for me, can you please speak to Daddy.

Mummy: What time do you have to go to get the vehicle?

Stephen: I will go by 11:00 A.M.

Mummy: What time is it now?

Stephen: 9:00 A.M. Mummy, can you please tell Daddy?

Mummy: Daddy has only lived all his life on his terms. He has always done what he felt was correct. He has never asked for opinions from anyone before he did anything. He has enjoyed all his life and has lived the way he liked. (*smiling*)

Stephen: So, shall I?

Mummy: It is your wish my dear; do what you think is best for you. I will always be there with you and will support you (*smiling*); but please try not to hurt your

Daddy. All my life I have obeyed whatever he has said, and he always lived like a king, and I don't want to see him sad and in shame at this age because of you. You are big enough to think and make a decision for yourself.

Stephen: Love you, Mummy. *(kissing on the forehead)*

Mummy: Love you too, Son.

Calling Caren

Stephen: I am in your showroom, where are you?

Caren: Hey, I am coming. Wait... (phone disconnected)

Caren came out of her cabin to greet me and all her staff stared at their boss's VIP guest.

Caren: Your vehicle is ready.

Stephen: Thank you for all the help, Caren; so are you free now? Shall we have lunch together?

Caren: I have brought lunch.

Stephen: Take your lunch along, we will eat that as well, is there a restaurant close by?

Caren: Yes, there is one nearby.

Stephen: Go get your food, let's eat.

Caren was shocked to see me eat her lunch while she ate from the restaurant.

Caren: Did you like it?

Stephen: Yes, very tasty; there was a time when I dreamt of you cooking food for me as my wife

Caren: I am sorry dear, sorry for everything.

After lunch I dropped her back to her office and bid her farewell; we both hugged each other and shook hands.

Stephen: Thanks for everything, Caren; never thought I would get this vehicle so fast and it is all because of you. Thanks. Daddy will bother you every time now with the service of this vehicle.

Caren: Tell Daddy that he can bother me whenever he wants; you take care of yourself and get married fast. I want to see you settled.

Stephen: Try to come with Robin and your baby if possible before I leave.

Caren: Let me see.

Stephen: Bye!

Caren: Bye!

I was driving my own car for the first time in Kerala. I have had many vehicles at home but I was never allowed to drive any of them. The rule was that only Daddy would drive. I was allowed to drive a bike later and that was it.

It was raining and I took the new vehicle to our church to get it blessed. I paid the fees and the priest blessed my vehicle. I walked to the cemetery to show my ancestors and my grandparents my new vehicle which I was going to give to their son. I prayed as usual at the grave and lit candles and while returning to my vehicle I saw Ann; this time I was not going to hide, I was not the old Stephen anymore and I decided to meet her.

Stephen: How are you, Ann.

Ann: All good, and you?

Stephen: Yeah, good

Ann: Came for vacation?

Stephen: Yeah, Mummy is not quite well.

Ann: I heard, how is she now?

Stephen: She is fine now, recovering.

Ann: Marriage plans?

Stephen: Not yet. (*smiling*)

Ann: Hmm...

Stephen: Alright, I need to go, see you later, nice to have met you.

Ann: New car?

Stephen: Yes!

Ann: Nice car.

Stephen: Thanks, it is for Daddy.

Ann: Ah, ok!

Stephen: So shall I leave? Do you want me to drop you somewhere?

Ann: That's fine I will manage.

Stephen: Ok then, bye.

Ann: Stephen, sorry for everything.

Stephen: Don't be silly, Ann, you did the right thing by obeying your parents; certain things are not meant to be.

Ann: Ok, bye.

Stephen: Bye, Ann.

I reached home that night content and happy and I was very happy to hand over the keys of the new car to my Daddy. He was like a small kid who got a new toy. I was happy that everyone around me was happy. There was nothing left to do now. I thanked my Lord for all the blessings; it was time now to start my life and for that, I had to get back to Dubai.

Rachel was back from Delhi. We spoke a lot but I could not go and see her in Bangalore, but we became good friends. I told her everything I wanted to tell her in all these years. I pulled out her picture from my purse and looked at it one last time and then threw it into the dustbin; I did not require it anymore.

I called Michelle, we spoke for quite some time; she was happy with her family.

I called the National Award winner Ziya before I left. She was in her own bubble as usual; wished her all success in life.

I left Kerala for the first time happy and content. I smiled for the first time while saying goodbye to my parents. I felt like a grown-up for the first time. I was no more a small boy, I was no more that cry baby.

I promised Daddy and Mummy that I would get married soon, but I had to set a few things right before that.

I kissed my parents before I left and said, "I love you, Daddy and Mummy. I love you both a lot."

Chapter 24

(*Phone call...*)

Stephen: Hi...

Clara: Hey, hi...when did you arrive?

Stephen: About an hour and a half...

Clara: Flight was on time?

Stephen: Yeah...

Clara: So, what else?

Stephen: I want to tell you something, it is a surprise. When are we meeting?

Clara: What is it, tell me?

Stephen: I will tell you when we meet.

Clara: When do you want to meet? Today?

Stephen: Tomorrow is Friday, right? Come to my place.

Clara: Oh, you have a place now. (*chuckles*) It's a studio?

Stephen: No, a one-bedroom hall.

Clara: Wow, not bad... All set to get married huh. (*grinning*)

Stephen: I will WhatsApp you the location map.

Clara: Yeah, sure.

Stephen: You will come in the morning itself right.

Clara: What are you up to? Why in the morning itself? (*grinning*)

Stephen: I am cooking so if you were here things would taste a little better? (*laughing*)

Clara: So you have a full set up, huh? I am impressed. Well, I can't promise anything. It depends on what time I wake up. I don't want to wake up early otherwise I will be grumpy.

Stephen: That's fine but we will have lunch together at my place, ok?

Clara: Ok, cool.

Stephen: Ok bye, catch up later.

Clara: Bye. (*phone disconnected*)

I wanted to prepare mutton biriyani for my lady, so I got all the ingredients for the same. I had ghee, onions, ginger, garlic, whole spices, and the regular spices powders with me in my kitchen. I had to buy fresh mutton, yogurt, mint leaves, coriander leaves, cashew nuts, saffron, rosewater, and of course the long grain basmati rice. I was quite a good cook, I prepared food on my own at the weekends.

I was shopping, and I reached the shelves which had medicines, condoms, and lubricants. I felt like buying a few things but I was hesitant, what if Clara would feel offended. I thought of buying a pack of condoms at least and picked a pack only to ditch it at the payment counter. I was not afraid if Clara got pregnant as I had made up my mind that she was going to be my wife. I had my mother's blessings and that was more than enough for me to get married to Clara.

That evening, I marinated the mutton cuts for the biriyani which I was going to prepare the next day. I was all ready for Clara.

That night was a long night for me, I could not wait for it to become morning, I could not wait to see Clara. I needed her in my life and I was going to convince her to be mine, to be my wife.

I picked up my phone to message her and that is when I saw that there were a few messages that had come a while ago.

I had a few messages from Bethany and I had a couple of messages from Rachel. I quickly opened Bethany's messages.

Bethany: Hi Stephen, hope you reached safely. I am organizing a small party at home tomorrow evening at my place, hope you can make it. Everyone in our department will be coming; I will send you the location map, please come in by 8:00 PM if possible.

Stephen: Yes all well, reached safely. I would have loved to come, but I have guests coming in tomorrow at my place; however, I will try to make it but I don't promise, anyway, thanks for the invitation.

Bethany: I will be expecting you, Stephen.

The last message from Bethany seemed like an order or command for me to be present there at her party, or was it that she had something to tell me?

Bethany was a very tough woman, she was quite the strict Manager type, but I always felt that she was making up that image for herself. She was more like being that harsh and loud woman to get respect or maybe because she wanted everyone to stay away from her. I always knew that she was soft from within. She used to treat me like a rag when I first joined, but gradually she started treating me with respect.

She was always working out, exercising at the gym. She sure had six-packs under her blouse, she was so fit that it literally showed. However, she was not a regular sports person like Ziya—slim and thin. Bethany was fit but at the same time she had good and firm fronts and curvy buttocks; she was the fight girl kind, the lady Croft of our office, very sexy but at the same time dangerously dangerous.

Rachel: Hi, Stephen, hope you reached there safely; it is boring here in Bangalore; waiting for my husband to come down and then after a few days we will all fly back to Canada.

Stephen: Hi, Rachel, yes, I reached safely, sorry for the delay in replying was just getting a few things done at my apartment.

Rachel: Hi, that's fine...glad you replied, I was kind of getting worried.

Stephen: I am so sorry for not being able to come and see you.

Rachel: Ah... don't worry, there is always a next time.

Stephen: When will your husband arrive?

Rachel: Tomorrow evening.

Stephen: How is your baby?

Rachel: She is fine.

Stephen: You alright? All well?

Rachel: Yeah, I am fine.

Stephen: You take care then Rachel, catch up later, good night.

Rachel: Sure, ok, good night.

When I needed Rachel the most in my life I never had her and today she was getting worried when she didn't see a message from me. Women are strange, complicated, and very difficult to understand.

People keep saying that women are the weaker sex, but I have always felt that woman is the most powerful of God's creations.

Later at night I sent a message to Clara.

Stephen: Hi, are you there?

Clara: Hi, yeah... Tell me.

Stephen: No, nothing, just waiting to see you tomorrow.

Clara: Same here!

Stephen: Come as soon as possible, ok.

Clara: Yeah, sure.

Stephen: Ok sleep now, good night.

Clara: Good night, Sweets.

The doorbell rings at about 9:00 A.M.; since it was Friday I had got up a little late than usual. I was having my coffee. I quickly opened the door and it was Clara. It was a surprise, I wanted her to come in early but she was in much earlier than I had expected. We both hugged each other, and the hug lasted for at least a minute, and when I looked at Clara's face she was crying. I wiped her tears and kissed her forehead. We sat on the sofa looking at each other, smiling for a few minutes. We never spoke anything to each other, there was silence in the room. Our eyes spoke so much, we were staring at each other and smiling, giggling like small kids; tears poured out of our eyes without any reason.

Clara: Is that coffee? (*wiping her tears*)

Stephen: Yes, you want some?

Clara: Yeah!

Stephen: Wait, I will make some for you.

Clara: No, I will have yours. (*quickly pulling my coffee mug*)

Stephen: Make yourself comfortable, I will go to the washroom and come back

Clara: Yeah, ok.

When I came out of the washroom, Clara had washed all the plates in the sink and she had made my bed as well.

Stephen: Wow, my house looks like a house now, by the way, that was quick. Thank you. Where is Zoyie?

Clara: She was fast asleep, so I could not bring her.

Stephen: Good.

Clara: Good?

Stephen: No... I mean good you didn't wake her.

Then I slowly went and sat next to Clara, she was going through the headlines in the newspaper, and since she was not paying attention to me I pushed myself closer to her and she quickly got up from the sofa and asked, "Can I use your washroom?"

Stephen: Sure!

Clara: I need a towel as well.

I pulled out a fresh towel from my cupboard and handed it over to Clara. She went into the washroom and I went into the kitchen to prepare some breakfast. I had bread, butter, and eggs so I decided to make bread toasts and some omelet for both of us. While I was toasting the bread, I heard my bathroom door open and then after a few minutes, Clara was in the kitchen with me. She was only wearing her top, she had removed her jeans, but she had her cycling shorts on; she had worn them inside her jeans. Clara was not her usual bubbly self, she was quiet; her eyes were red and so I asked her, "Were you crying?"

Clara: No my dear, you go and sit in the hall, I will make breakfast...

Stephen: No, I want to be with you.

I saw Clara preparing breakfast and I kept looking at her thighs and her beautiful body.

Clara noticed that I was checking her out and she said, "Go and sit in the hall, it is quite warm in the kitchen, I will bring the breakfast in a few minutes."

I could not control myself and I put my hands around Clara's waist from behind; Clara quickly pulled my hands apart and said, "Stephen, please... Don't touch me."

Stephen: What happened, Clara?

Clara: Nothing, just stay away from me... Please.

Clara was not angry when she told me that, she was more like pleading with me. I told myself that may be she needed sometime to get used to me again as it had been quite some time that we had met each other.

We had breakfast together and Clara made some more coffee for us.

Clara: Can I sleep for some time, my head is paining

Stephen: Sure!

She went into the bedroom and I heard her speaking to Zoyie over the phone. *Mumma will be back soon baby, don't worry.*

I decided to start working on my biriyani as it was about 11:30 A.M. already, and I started preparing the same. Biriyani came out quite nicely, better than I had expected and I went to the bedroom to see if Clara was ok.

Clara was fast asleep. I looked at her for some time and I got onto the bed and slept next to her; I thought she would get up but she was fast asleep, I hugged her from behind, but she was still asleep, her breasts were touching my arms. I slowly placed my hand on one of her breasts, and she quickly woke up. She was kind of shocked and scared and she looked at me and I quickly understood that I had startled her.

Stephen: I am sorry, very sorry to have woken you up.

Clara: That's ok... (*sighing, and breathing hard*)

Stephen: You ok, right?

Clara: hmm... (*indicating that she was fine*) What time is it?

Stephen: It is 2:00 P.M., lunch is ready.

Clara: Wow, it smells amazing. Let's eat, I am hungry.

Stephen: Sure!

While we both got out of bed I tried to hug Clara. she never resisted the hug and then I tried to kiss her lips but she turned her face. I held her face in my hands and gave it a second try but then she again turned her face in the other direction. I got irritated and tried the third time, with a little bit of force, but this time she pushed me off and walked into the kitchen. I went to the kitchen and Clara was all busy opening the dum of the biriyani. The smell of saffron and rosewater was pouring out of the vessel, and she was praising me for the biriyani I had made. She quickly made some raita to go with the biriyani with the few vegetables she could find in my fridge. We both ate the biriyani. Clara cleared the kitchen in no time; washed all the dishes and arranged my untidy kitchen as well.

While we relaxed watching the TV, I put my hands on her hands, but she never pushed my hands away; after a few minutes, she asked me, "Shall we go out?"

Stephen: I have to go to this party my manager is hosting at her place.

Clara: What time do you have to go?

Stephen: I need to be there by 7:00 P.M.

Clara: Oh... ok; well I will leave then, you carry on... (*she quickly got up and went into the bedroom*)

I went behind her into the bedroom, she was going to put on her jeans when I went behind her and hugged her. I could not resist anymore and I started kissing behind her neck and I started caressing her breasts, she was trying to push me off, she said in a soft voice "*no, please*" but there was no stopping. I had already made up my mind, I wanted to make love to my future wife. I wanted to tell her that my Mummy was ok with our relationship and that I did not care about anyone else, but she was resisting my moves. I quickly put my hand inside her cycling shorts; she quickly caught my hand pulled it out of her shorts and turned around and pushed me off and said, "I told you to stop right, what is gone wrong with you? You don't own me Stephen and I don't owe you anything." *(bursting into tears)*

I was shocked...

Stephen: What happened? Why are you crying, my dear? It is me Stephen! Why are you behaving like this?

Clara: You are also just like the others, you want to fuck me right? Come on then... Do it fast, do whatever you want. *(she slept on the bed crying)*

Stephen: What are you doing? Just get up and stop this, stop crying. I wanted to tell you that Mummy is very much happy and is on our side, she wants us to get married; I don't want anyone else's permission. I need you, Clara, let's just get married. I will take care of Zoyie like my own daughter. We will face everything together, please, Clara. For your information your ex-husband is in jail for some fraud case here in Abu Dhabi, I am sure no court any where in the world is now going to allow him custody of Zoyie anymore.

Clara on hearing my words started crying even more. She started crying uncontrollably with her head on my chest, hugging me; and I kept apologizing to her and trying to console and convince her to get married to me.

After some time, she got up from the bed, got dressed, and was all set to leave and I asked her...

You never gave me an answer Clara.

Clara: Let's speak about this later please, I need to go now.

Stephen: Clara, this is my life and I am very serious, I need an answer from you.

Clara: I love you, Stephen, I love you more than anything, but I am not the right person for you. I have nothing to give you my love. I am no good for you. You have a bright future, someone will come into your life.

Stephen: Please stop this nonsense, can't you see? All my friends are already married, it is just me, and I can't be with anyone else except you. I just can't see anyone else in the place of my wife other than you, so, please...

Clara: I need to go, bye. (*she walked out of my house*)

Stephen: Clara, please... Clara!

That evening I went to Bethany's party. I was not quite in the mood, everyone in our department was present. There was food, snacks, and drinks. I sat in a corner, quietly. There was a storm within me. Bethany knowing that I was upset called me to her balcony where there was no one and she asked me what the matter was. I told her everything about Clara and our relationship; and then Bethany said, "You need to go and get your girl Stephen before it is too late; I am a woman and I know for sure that she is fighting a battle within her, and each time she is giving you a 'no' she is in more pain; why don't you go to her place now and sort this out; finish it for good. You are one of the best negotiators I have ever seen, and I want you to use your skills; do you want me to come along with you?"

Stephen: No, I will manage.

Bethany: Just go Stephen before it is too late.

I just hugged Bethany and thanked her and left the party. I got into my car and looked at my watch, it was almost 9:30 P.M. I quickly sent a message to Clara.

I am coming to your place, now; I need you and Zoyie in my life. I will speak to your family.

I drove like a mad man to her place, there were mixed feelings within me. I was confused and afraid—afraid of getting rejected again, afraid that her family would make fun of me and would insult me. I quickly called my Mummy on the way, and I told her that I was going to Clara's place and Mummy replied, "I will be praying for you my Son, go and do what you think is right for you; I will be with you always and wait Daddy wants to speak to you..."

Daddy: It is your life, Son, we will be with you in whatever you decide. If it is Clara that you love then go and get her my Son, all the best, and may God Bless You. *(phone disconnected)*

I immediately felt brave and I was not afraid anymore. I had my Mummy's blessings and my Daddy's prayers, and so I parked my vehicle below her apartment and walked up to her place and I pressed the calling bell, the door was opened by Celin Aunty. *(Clara's elder sister)*

Celin Aunty: Come in, glad you made it. *(in a soft voice, as though she was expecting me)*

Looking at my puzzled face...

Celin Aunty: Didn't you get my messages?

Stephen: No, I didn't see...

Celin Aunty: You love her right? And you want to marry her?

Stephen: Yes, Aunty.

Celin Aunty: So you understand the fact that you will have to take Zoyie also into your life when you marry Clara, right?

Stephen: Yes, Aunty, I know all that.

And suddenly James Uncle (*Celin Aunty's husband, and Clara's brother-in-law*) came into the scene interrupting our conversation and said in an angry tone.

James Uncle: So you are the one who wants to marry my girl, huh?

Celin Aunty: Clara is not your girl, you are supposed to consider her as your own sister

James Uncle: You bitch! Shut up and get lost, I am speaking to this asshole, what is your age, huh?

Celin Aunty: Please don't spoil my sister's life. (*pleading with folded hands in front of her husband*)

Stephen: What is happening here where is Clara?

Celin Aunty: This man (*pointing at James Uncle*) tried to rape Clara yesterday night; luckily myself and my father reached at the right time or else my sister would have been ruined... (*burst into tears*)

James Uncle immediately walked up in front of me and slapped me and asked me to get out of their house. I did not retaliate but asked...

Stephen: Where is Clara? (*in a soft but angry tone*)

Celin Aunty: She is in her room.

I walked up to Clara's room and called out...

Stephen: Clara open the door, it is me, Stephen...

And the door to Clara's room opened, Clara had packed her bags and was ready with Zoyie.

Stephen: You had this storm within you and you never told me anything?

Clara quickly hugged me and started crying. It was only then that I understood as to why she wouldn't let me touch her in the morning. I apologized to Clara and kissed her, and I caught both her and Zoyie's hands and walked towards Celin Aunty.

Stephen: I am taking them both... I will call you.

James again came towards me to fight and then Clara said–

Clara: If you touch him one more time, I will file a complaint to the police and then you will be finished, so don't you dare. I did not do that all this while only for my sister, it takes only a phone call. You know this country, right? You will be finished if I tell everything to the police, so stay away.

Clara's and Celin Auntie's Dad (father) walked in hearing all this; he quietly came to me and hugged me and said, "Take my little girl... God Bless you, my Son."

The three of us walked out of that house that night. I got my girl that night. We got married soon in Kerala. Mummy was very happy, and Daddy accepted our relationship. A few of my relative thought that the lady I got married to was Rachel; some of them thought that Clara was a millionaire and that was the reason why I got married to her even though she had a child; some made fun of me saying "he has got a free child with the bride". These people never knew that only my Clara was there when I was alone, the so-called relatives and friends only watched from a distance.

I was happy. I had Clara and Zoyie my daughter. I was proud that I got the most beautiful girl I could ever get. She was the most dynamic woman, I had ever known and most of all she was very understanding and we had no secrets between us.

I was finally married to the girl I loved. I was married to the girl who taught me the names of cars. I was married to the girl who taught me how to make love. I loved her more than anything. The Lord had answered my prayes at last; he gave me the best after all.

Chapter 25

Present-day...

Knocking at the door of our bedroom...

Zoyie: Is Maa awake?

Stephen: No, she is sleeping, but you can come in, Zoyie...

Zoyie went near Clara and kissed her good morning

Clara: Today is a Friday, guys! Both father and daughter are the same, why don't you guys sleep for some more time. *(laughing)*

Zoyie: Maa, why you are naked always in the mornings, why don't you put on some clothes?

Clara: Ask your father.

Stephen: Zoyie, it is very hot right that's why she sleeps like that...

Clara: Yeah...yeah (giggling);

Zoyie exits the bedroom (giggling) and goes to her room...

Stephen: She must have understood, right?

Clara: Sure she did, she is not a small girl. She knows everything, but don't worry she is very understanding. Hey, what are you drinking?

Stephen: Sulaimani. I had to make it on my own, I don't have anybody to even make me a cup of sulaimani. (*teasing*)

Clara: Really? (*smiling*), my dear husband, you hardly let me sleep last night and you want sulaimani early in the morning huh. (*laughing*) And that too you need it in style, with saffron and rosewater. And what did you say, I sleep without clothes because I feel hot huh? (*laughing*)

Stephen: You are hot my love and I like you without clothes. (*grinning*) I would have never allowed you to wear any clothes if it was possible; so, shall we have one more round?

Clara: no, please... My body is aching. I am not as young as you love; you have married a woman who is much older than you so please handle me with care. (laughing)

Stephen: Oh sure! (grinning) I slowly walked to the door and locked it and got in between the sheets with Clara.

Life becomes even more beautiful when we have the people whom we love in our lives. It is not all the time about money, fame, or being successful in our careers. I have seen the money come and go in life. I have experienced the best and the worst in life as well, and all I can say is that love is better than anything in this world and love is all that we need and what matters.

www.ingramcontent.com/pod-product-compliance
Lightning Source LLC
Chambersburg PA
CBHW020908160726
47993CB00005B/1879